A
Harlequin
Romance

A GARLAND OF MARIGOLDS

by

ISOBEL CHACE

HARLEQUIN BOOKS   TORONTO
WINNIPEG

First published in 1967 by Mills & Boon Limited,
50 Grafton Way, Fitzroy Square, London, England.

Harlequin Canadian edition published October, 1967
Harlequin U.S. edition published January, 1968

Reprinted 1971
Reprinted 1972

Printed in Canada

CHAPTER ONE

ON the day I got my degree Timothy took me out to dinner. Tonight, I thought, as we strolled along the Embankment beside the Thames, he would ask me to marry him, and of course I was going to accept. We had been to a Chinese restaurant and the food had not agreed with Timothy's delicate digestion, but he had plied me with enough wine to sink a ship, which wasn't very fair because while I was now in a happy glow, he was as sober as ever.

"What you ought to do is go abroad," he said suddenly.

I pulled his arm closer around my shoulders, marvelling at the way his bones seemed to stick through his flesh as if he were little fatter than a skeleton.

"Abroad?" I repeated blithely. "Whatever for?"

He looked at me sorrowfully. "I should have thought that you would be longing to share your knowledge with the under-privileged," he explained.

I reached up a hand and pulled at his ear. "How can you be so earnest on a night like this?" I asked placidly.

He winced in pain, more from his indigestion than from any action of mine.

"The world today is a thing to be earnest about!" he retorted.

"Nonsense!" I stopped walking and wandered towards the stone parapet to watch a string of barges going past, behind a squat busy little tug snorting under the effort it was making. "Why should I want to leave all this?" I demanded. And to tell the truth it was all very beautiful. The Thames looked dark and powerful that night, hazing in the distance into evening mist. A few lights had come on and it was already dark enough for them to be repeated in the water. Even the more terrible of the new match-box architecture, international and yet a foreigner in almost every land, was softened in the changing hour to more reasonable proportions.

At the back of my mind I was trying to decide how I was going to make Timothy kiss me before we got home. He was surprisingly shy about showing his affection in public and was constantly worried about what other people might think of his choice in tailoring and ties as his mother had once convinced him that it was on these things that one was judged for the rest of one's life. It was the one drawback I knew of in our relationship.

Timothy stared moodily at the Houses of Parliament, allowing his eyes to travel slowly down the river to where we were standing.

"Suki," he said at last, "I've been trying to tell you all evening. I'm going to the States."

At first I didn't believe him.

"I suppose you're going to be an astronaut!" I teased him. Timothy was a space scientist and was madly interested in blasting useless objects into the sky at vast expense, but then I'm prejudiced because I always have thought that the moon was a dead bore outside of its proper romantic place.

He smiled thinly.

"It's to do with rockets, certainly. Part of the brain drain, I suppose," he added, half laughing.

I regarded him petulantly.

"But *I* don't want to go to America!" I complained.

Timothy looked wretchedly embarrassed and he coughed to clear his throat.

"No, I know. Actually I shall only be gone for two years. It's a great experience for me, but they do stipulate an unmarried man. I thought we might put off any proper engagement until I got back."

It was a very bitter blow. Now that I was qualified, I felt I was ready to be married. I had even turned down a couple of very nice jobs for that very reason. Timothy and I belonged together and, besides anything else, he needed looking after, with proper meals at proper times and a loving wife to mix his stomach potions for him and to comfort him when his chronic indigestion really got the upper hand.

"I suppose," I said in a voice which trembled despite all my best efforts, "I might be able to get a job near by."

Timothy bit his lip.

"But that's the whole point! I can't afford to have any distractions while I'm over there—and you are rather a distraction to me! We've been seeing too much of each other lately and we both need time to think. That's why I think you ought to go abroad too."

I swallowed dismally.

"But we are going to get married eventually, aren't we?"

He brushed away the question as being of limited importance.

"I suppose so. But we need these two years to *know*. Let's see what happens, shall we?"

I tossed my head, my pride coming to my rescue.

"And no strings attached?" I asked him lightly.

He grinned, patently relieved that I had not burst into tears or done anything else to make him feel uncomfortable.

"No strings attached," he agreed.

And so I did not become Mrs. Timothy Black that summer. I remained plain Miss Susan King. However, I did pack Timothy's clothes and possessions for him and saw him off at the airport, receiving a peck on my cheek for my pains. When it was all over, I went to the nearest self-service café and ate a horrid mixture of sausages and spaghetti, before going home and crying myself to sleep.

The following day I decided to go to India.

The advertisement had not been particularly attractive. It had read more like a University joke. From it I gathered that someone wished to employ somebody with my qualifications in an experimental village at somewhere quite unpronounceable in India. There was, the advertisement had gone on to say, an experimental irrigation scheme which watered the main farm. The newcomer would be trying out various new wheat and maize hybrids to find out which would do best locally. He, or she, would be paid a pittance for this privilege and would also have to prove that their qualifications were better than any Indian national's who cared to apply. Perhaps it was because it sounded so hopeless that I applied for a job. It was at least in India, which was where I had decided to go, and as it didn't sound in any sense a particularly attractive job, there was every chance that nobody else would apply for it.

Nobody else did. I received a reply to my letter asking me to ring up a Mr. Gideon Wait at a Putney number, and a sense of excitement gripped me and, for the first time, I went to sleep without even thinking about Timothy and wondering what he was doing.

The telephone was answered by the young fresh voice of a girl.

"Camilla Wait," she said softly, breathing the name caressingly into the receiver in a way which must have taken a lot of practice.

"Is your father there?" I asked her.

There was a moment's complete silence, then her voice came again, more wary and not a little curious.

"No, he isn't. As a matter of fact he never has lived here."

A prickle of exasperation travelled through me.

"I was told to telephone this number—" I began crisply.

"Ah yes!" Camilla agreed. "But it's Gideon you want to speak to. He's my brother."

I made a quick mental revision of her possible age. I had decided before that she was about sixteen, now I began to wonder if she were older.

"Is he *there*?" I asked her and explained who I was. She giggled, quite unabashed.

"No, he's not. Look," she went on gaily, "the best thing is for you to come round this evening and have something to eat with us. Gideon is sure to be here part of the time." She gave me the address and a few rather wild directions as how to get there, then I put down the receiver and dashed across to the wardrobe to see what I could find to wear. Anyone would have thought that Gideon Wait meant something to me personally and, in a way, he did. He was the first man I had eaten with since Timothy had gone to America, and I felt as shy and as involved as if he were my first date. Looking at myself in the looking-glass, I thought I had allowed myself to get into a fine mess. I wasn't particularly tall, but I held myself well, giving an impression of more inches than I actually possessed. I had dark, unruly hair and a nose which couldn't be ignored over a wide, mobile mouth that usually gave expression to my normal cheerfulness. There was no doubt that the new lipstick I had recently brought was a great success, and it exactly matched the wispy scarf I intended to tie round my neck, which would look better still. No, it wasn't my looks I was worried about. It was this new vulnerability that Timothy had left me heir to. I no longer felt on top of the situation.

I felt progressively less confident as the bus lurched over Putney Bridge in the general direction that Camilla had told me to go. Supposing I didn't like India? Supposing I couldn't manage the job? Or, even more important, supposing I didn't like Mr. Wait, the man who seemed to be in charge of the experimental farm? I got off the bus in a dream, telling myself how foolish it was to worry, and only succeeding in worrying all the more, as one always does.

I found the house quite easily. It was one of those comfortable, old-fashioned London houses that are solidly elegant and sometimes still have the bars on the nursery windows on the top floor. Mostly they have all been turned into flats in these less spacious days, but every now and again one sees one full of children and fun and, more often than not, with peeling painted façades that are hopefully being left yet another year before they are finally 'done up'. The Wait house was one of these. It was actually Gideon's house, but his sister and her family lived there as he was abroad so much. Usually there were half a dozen other people there was well, but who they all were I was never able to discover.

I walked up the few steps to the front door and rang the bell. It was a long time before anyone came, and I was on the point of ringing again when the door slowly opened and a small voice said :

"Will you come in and tell me why you've come?"

I stared down at the small child who was firmly shutting the door behind me. It was impossible to tell if it was a boy or a girl as its hair was cut as short as possible and it was dressed in a shirt and jeans.

"Hullo," I said.

The child glowered up at me.

"That's no answer. Whom have you come to see?"

"Mr. Wait," I said, feeling rather squashed.

"Oh," the child said wisely. "Uncle Gideon. He's out, but Camilla wants to see you. She wants to make sure you're the right person before Uncle Gideon sees you. He'll take anyone who seems keen, you see."

"And that matters?" I asked faintly.

The child chuckled, and I was almost sure he was a boy.

"He's had a couple of stumers!" he told me. "Camilla says it's all his own fault because he's no judge of character."

"And Camilla is?" I asked a shade tartly.

The child nodded solemnly.

"There are no flies on Camilla."

He showed me into the sitting-room, still smiling in that quiet, superior manner that told me he was quite sure that Camilla was going to take complete control of the interview no matter what I chose to do about it. If he was a typical Wait, I thought darkly, the sooner I left the better. I was too sore from my recent experiences with Timothy to want to indulge in personal relationships with anyone else of any age. I was in a mood to be careful, and if I could avoid doing so, I wasn't going to let even this youngster trespass on my affections.

Camilla took me by surprise. She came hesitantly into the room and paused on the threshold, whispering an apology for her freshly washed hair and the state of her clothes.

"I was bathing the children," she explained. "My younger nephews and nieces. Their mother is out."

I cleared my throat.

"Are there—are there many of them?" I asked.

Camilla grinned. "Four altogether," she said cheerfully. "Two of them are twins." She sat down on the chair opposite mine, her deep blue eyes taking in every detail of my appearance. I returned stare for stare, trying to make up my mind if she were as nice and as young as she looked.

"Will your brother be in soon?" I asked at last.

Camilla had the grace to look guilty.

"Perhaps you would like to stay for supper?" she asked.

"Very much!" I agreed warmly. "Does he know I'm even coming?" I went on in conversational tones.

Camilla shook her head.

"I know it's awful of me, but Gideon is so stupid about getting people to go to India. An ounce of good will and he's convinced they're the answer to his prayers!"

I laughed. "And they are not?"

"They haven't been so far. He hasn't had anyone stay longer than six weeks!"

My heart sank. Was it such a terribly hard job, with so few rewards?

"I'm not sure I shall do any better," I said aloud. "I've never been out of England before."

Camilla looked thoughtful.

"I think you'll do very nicely," she said light-heartedly. "You're not going to rush off and get married or anything awful, are you?"

I winced. "No," I replied sharply. "There's no danger of that!"

Camilla's eyes gleamed with amusement.

"Congratulations, Miss King," she teased me. "I shall give you a drink to celebrate!" She went over to a cupboard and produced an array of bottles. "What will you have? Gin? Sherry?"

I chose a dry sherry and watched her as she carefully poured it out for me.

"Are you going to have one?" I asked.

She laughed, glancing at me over her shoulder.

"Me? Gideon would be horrified! I'm only here at all because I'm in the middle of changing schools. And after that I still have to be finished!" she added with a horrible grimace.

"I see," I said, not seeing at all. "I thought you were about the age to leave school."

"I am," she retorted. "Only Gideon has this thing about education. I would be far more use to him in India. Who wants to be finished?"

"Wouldn't you like to go to university?" I asked her, remembering my own struggles to get an education, remembering too with gratitude the sacrifices my parents had made to make it possible.

"I haven't the brains," she admitted cheerfully. "Gideon says it's marriage or stagnation for me. Apparently gentlemen prefer ' finished blondes—"

"What nonsense !" I interrupted her brusquely.

She laughed. "Isn't it?" A sudden idea struck her, transforming her face into an expression of angelic consideration. "I suppose you wouldn't like to persuade Gideon that India would be much more broadening to the mind?"

"No, I wouldn't," I answered firmly. "But your parents—?"

"They're dead," she replied simply. "They died when I was quite small. Gideon and Rachel, my sister, have practically brought me up. The last word is always Gideon's, though, because he pays the bills !"

I looked down at my glass of sherry, astonished by the sudden soft warmness inside me. Gideon sounded nice, and so perhaps life was not so bad. Perhaps even two years would not be too long to wait for Timothy.

"It's a great pity," said Camilla.

Camilla and I put the children to bed. The twins, the youngest, were warm and sweet-smelling from their bath and were no trouble at all. They were not in the least put out at having a stranger to tuck them in and to tell them a long and involved story that pleased me as much as it did them. Camilla had the more difficult task with her niece and the small boy, Jeffrey, who had let me in to the house. The sun was setting when we had finished and a red glow shone over London in a pink and mysterious twilight. Camilla shut it firmly out by drawing the curtains and lighting the lamps. At night, I thought, the drawing-room took on an added elegance because one could no longer see the worn materials that covered the chairs nor the frayed edges of the glowing curtains.

We had only just sat down when we heard a key scrape in the lock of the front door.

"That will be Gideon," Camilla informed me with satisfaction.

I barely had time to gather myself together before the door opened and a larger, incredibly masculine edition of Camilla came into the room. He was fair as she was, with the same well-shaped bones and the same jutting firmness round the chin. He started when he saw me and looked enquiringly at Camilla.

"This is Susan King," his young sister said briefly. "She's going with you to India."

Gideon's face darkened with annoyance.

"Are the children in bed?" he asked abruptly.

"Of course," Camilla answered coolly.

"Then go and find yourself something else to do!" he snapped at her. She rose in one easy movement and went towards the door, winking at me behind his back.

"Susan is staying for supper," she said from the doorway.

"Susan?" he repeated testily.

"Actually," I said, feeling rather sorry about Camilla's curt dismissal, "most people call me Suki. Susan is only for formal occasions."

"Miss King," he said icily, "I hope Camilla has not given you the wrong impression, but I shall need to know a great deal more about you before I decide whether or not you will be suitable for the job I have to offer."

My feeling of warm security fell away from me. I was as cold as I had been ever since I had said goodbye to Timothy.

"Of course," I said.

Gideon frowned over the list of my qualifications and the two letters of reference I had brought him. It was impossible to tell whether he was satisfied or not.

"What made you think of India?" he asked abruptly.

I tried desperately to think of my reasons.

"I have the knowledge," I stammered. "I thought I could be useful."

He looked up at me and his eyes were a dark, dark blue that was very nearly black.

"You have the knowledge," he agreed. "But there's a great deal more to this job than that. Can you *teach* what you know?"

"I've never tried," I admitted. I was beginning to see why none of his other assistants had lasted for longer than six weeks. He obviously expected them to work miracles on absolutely nothing at all! Even the marked likeness between Gideon and his sister faded into insignificance as I thought about how much I disliked him.

Gideon tossed my papers impatiently back on to my knees.

"And then you're a woman!" he said crossly.

I sat up very straight, sure now that I was going to lose my temper.

"Do I have to apologise for that too?" I asked smoothly.

He swung round and surveyed my angry face, surprised that I should have declared battle. His eyes were suddenly amused.

"No," he said slowly, "I don't think you have to apologise for that!" His appreciation was even more unwelcome than his criticism as he added: "No, no apologies needed, I think!"

I was silent. Somehow he still had me at a disadvantage and I was resentful of the fact.

"You have to admit," he went on more gently, "that your sex makes certain administrative difficulties. The village is very much on the open plan scheme of living!"

I blushed. "I'll try not to be too obtrusive, Mr. Wait," I said primly.

"I shall see that you aren't!" he retorted. He grinned suddenly and I was aware that I had been accepted.

"You'd better ask me what you want to know about the place."

I hardly knew where to begin. "I know very little about India," I said.

He smiled, and I could see a very clear likeness to Camilla.

"That might be a great deal better than knowing an awful lot," he said dryly. "All you'll have to do is produce a bonanza crop of maize!"

In spite of myself I laughed, remembering what Camilla had thought of his previous assistants.

"Yes, sir," I said.

There was a soft knock at the door, followed almost immediately by Camilla.

"All fixed up? How very satisfactory!"

Her brother grabbed her by the hair. "You were listening at the door!" he accused her.

Camilla managed to look dignified if slightly resentful.

"Of course. Now all we have to decide is when we're leaving—"

Gideon stopped her with a look.

"You, young lady, are going back to school."

Camilla made a face at him. "That's what you think!" she growled. "I'm not a child any longer!"

"Then don't behave like a spoiled brat!"

Outraged, Camilla turned to me for support.

"Suki, isn't he impossible! Tell him I'm going with you to India. Tell him you *need* me! You'll need another woman about the place, won't you?" She ended with a shriek as Gideon took a tighter grip on her hair. "Let me go, you brute!"

"I think," I remarked loudly to no one in particular, "that Camilla behaves with great dignity and restraint."

Gideon Wait turned on me. "Are you backing her up, by any chance?"

"Well," I temporised. I had only just got the job and

I didn't want to lose it before I ever saw India. "She does seem a little old for school."

"She's seventeen! She only just scraped through her O levels. Why, she has hardly any education at all!"

"I don't think she'll need much," I said firmly. "She isn't the academic type. She put the children to bed very nicely and she probably does lots of things very well indeed—"

"And I'm not in the least interested in the period of Queen Anne!" Camilla finished for me. "She's dead!"

Gideon looked from one to the other of us and laughed.

"Very well," he yelled at us. "She can come to India! But she'll be *your* responsibility!" He poked an accusing finger in my direction before hugging his sister to him. Helplessly I watched them, wondering what I had taken on. Camilla was really very young and sweet, and surely she couldn't come to very much harm in an obscure village in India?

Camilla held out her hand to me to include me in the little group.

"How nice that you're staying on for supper," she said.

Packing was a nightmare. The days were full enough. If I had had any gaps, Camilla obligingly filled them with her endless questions and even more endless lists of the things she considered quite essential to take with her. Daily, I drastically pruned the pile of things I had decided to take myself, and daily I tried to persuade her to do the same thing. But Camilla was already one of those women who either travel with nothing more than a pocket handkerchief or else with at least ten bulging trunks. Nothing in between appealed to her, and only Gideon's flat refusal to take her with him at all produced a more reasonable list of her requirements.

But at night I was alone and I would wander through the streets of London, retracing the walks I had taken with Timothy. Down that cul-de-sac, beneath the third street lamp on the right, he had kissed me once, and I would remember and weep. It seemed so strange that he should now be in a different country and I should be going to India. In the daytime two years seemed a very short space of time, but in the evenings it would stretch itself out into eternity and I would even doubt that I should ever see Timothy again.

A tin of his stomach powder stood drunkenly on the top of a row of books beside my bed and I hadn't the heart to throw it away. Every day I would search the table down below, where all the tenants' letters were thrown, looking for a letter from him, but none came. He was settling in, I told myself. He was working hard and his tummy was probably upset by the change of food. I could almost see him before me, wincing in pain because of something he had eaten, and he was very dear to me. Sometimes it occurred to me to wonder why he had not kissed me more often before he had gone, but I wouldn't allow myself to ask the question very often. Timothy Black was an ascetic man who seldom allowed his feelings to get the better of him, and that strong puritanical streak had undoubtedly told him that it was wrong to even casually caress a woman to whom you were not yet married. And I couldn't complain, for it was partly this boyish diffidence and exaggerated respect which I had loved. It was only very occasionally that I could see that it was not so much respect for me, but a fear lest he should become emotionally involved in anything outside himself and his work. But this I would never admit. Why should I? I had enough warmth for the two of us! And barriers in love were only made to be broken down!

I cried a great deal in the nights before we left for India and I thought I grew plainer every day. Gideon thought so too.

"What's the matter with you?" he demanded curtly

one day, when he came across me lurking in his hall-way.

"I—I'm sorry," I had apologised.

He had put a hand on my shoulder and propelled me towards the light.

"I thought so! Burning the candle at both ends, I suppose? Camilla has more sense. You'd better get some colour in your cheeks before we go or I shall be tempted to leave you behind!"

"It's none of your business if I'm a bit pale!" I had retorted sharply.

His fingers had dug into my shoulder.

"Oh, isn't it? Well, I'm making it my business!" he had told me, his voice harsh with exasperation. "Are you ill, or are you letting your emotions get the better of you?"

I had swallowed. "Someone I know has gone to America," I had told him woodenly. "It's left a bit of a gap, I suppose."

To my surprise he had been quite kind.

"You'll get over it," he had said roughly. He had smiled down at me and his dark eyes had been warm and friendly. "He probably isn't worth all the misery."

I had smiled myself. "It's temporary misery," I had said quietly. "He'll be back in two years."

"And you're waiting for him?"

Too honest to lie, I had shaken my head.

"There are no strings attached," I had said abruptly. His sympathy had died and he had looked amused.

"Well, let's thank heavens for small mercies!" he had exclaimed. He had flicked my cheek with his finger. "You're not much older than Camilla, are you?"

Indignantly, I had regarded him with something approaching hatred. I wished passionately that I hadn't told him anything at all.

"Does it matter?" I had asked him languidly. "As long as I can grow maize?"

His laughter had rung through the house.

"Not a rap!" he had agreed.

And Timothy did seem to matter less the nearer we got to the day of our departure. On the last day, when we finally shut the suitcases we were taking with us on the aeroplane and said goodbye to our families and friends, I never thought about him at all. The only emotion I was aware of as we made our way to the airport was a burning sense of anticipation coupled with a juvenile feeling of panic that I was bound to lose either my passport or my ticket. Oh, whoops, I thought, India, here I come!

CHAPTER TWO

MOTHER INDIA! I pressed my nose against the awkward window and tried to see Delhi beyond the enormous grey wheeling wing of the aeroplane. The whole of India had been surprising to me from the air. There was so much empty space and huge outcrops of rocks that I supposed grew gradually higher and higher as they travelled north to the Himalayas. Somehow I had always imagined the sub-continent to be crammed full of people and very little else.

I hardly felt it at all when we actually landed and taxied across the concrete apron. Like all the other passengers, I struggled to my feet, smiling at my stiffness from sitting still and trying frantically to find all my hand luggage. Camilla and Gideon were on the other side of the enormous aircraft. They looked almost comically alike as he leaned towards his sister and cracked a joke in her ear. She glanced across at me and laughed, and I was annoyed to discover that I was hurt. It was one thing to be excluded from their family group, it was quite another to be the butt of their humour. But that was what I had to expect for the next two years, I reminded myself grimly. I would be one alone and that was the way I wanted it. I thought hard about Timothy with an increasing sense of panic as I realised that already his features were a trifle blurred in my mind and the pain of memory could no longer be made to ache on order.

The doors were flung open and the incredible heat from the outside rushed into the body of the plane. The sunlight danced in a haze of heat along the edge of the concrete, striking our feet even through the leather of our shoes. Camilla grimaced at me and made her way round a couple of static passengers to my side.

"Super flight!" she exclaimed ecstatically.

"Yes, I suppose it was," I agreed.

She grinned, not taken in for a minute by my lack of enthusiasm.

"For someone who dragged me round Rome for the greater part of the night, that must be the understatement of all time!" she teased me.

I looked around the airport buildings. "It doesn't seem very—Indian," I objected.

Her eyes danced. "You wait! Gideon has been telling me such stories about the people in the village that I can hardly wait to get there! He says we shall have to sleep on the local string beds and we're lucky to have them! *That* sounds Indian and sort of ascetic, doesn't it?"

I laughed. "Very!" I agreed amiably.

"Ah, here he comes!" she went on happily. "I suppose it's the Customs next." Her eyes fell on a group of Indian women dressed in colourful, flowing saris. "There," she exclaimed, prodding me in the ribs, "there's some local colour for you!"

Gideon's dark eyes met mine.

"Disappointed already?" he asked me smoothly.

I flushed. "It isn't that," I assured him hastily, but he wasn't even listening. He had taken off his coat and he walked off across the apron, swinging it easily between his fingers. The heat which had already reduced my crisp cotton frock to a rag apparently had no effect either on him or his clothes.

Camilla and I followed more slowly, determined not to miss anything. A couple of men, dressed in jodhpur trousers and long coat, stood in sober conversation by the entrance to the Customs. Beyond them was a wild character, his hair uncut and unbrushed, and his clothing no more than a sheet knotted over one shoulder. His staring eyes gave him the appearance of madness, but I thought he might be no more than a holy man and walked the long way round him just in case.

It was only when I had achieved my object that I realised that Gideon was watching me. It was too late then to pretend that I had not noticed the holy man or the indescribable odour that came from his body, but I put a brave face on it, hoping that the disapproval on Gideon's face was my imagination. It was not.

"Perhaps you and Camilla had better go outside while I see to the formalities," he said sharply.

Determined, I shook my head.

"I'd rather make sure of my own luggage," I said coldly.

We stood facing each other like a couple of boxers looking for an opening.

"What's the matter with you two?" Camilla asked us, puzzled.

Feeling rather foolish, I turned away and began to walk with her towards the street entrance. A row of taxis had drawn up outside the entrance. The chauffeurs squatted in a circle, gossiping the time away. They looked up when I showed myself in the doorway, jumping to their feet and running towards me, each one anxious that I should choose his cab. I moved back again out of sight and they gathered round the door, waiting, their eyes impassive.

At that moment another car drew up outside and a fair young man, so obviously American that I couldn't help smiling, came rushing into the reception lounge. He went straight across to Gideon and slapped him across the shoulders.

"So you're back!"

Gideon swung round, a wide smile on his face.

"And not alone!"

The American glanced about him with interest. "Anyone I know?"

Gideon beckoned to his sister and introduced the young man to her.

"Camilla, my love, this is my assistant, Joseph Groton. Joseph, my young sister. I brought her after all!"

The American shook her warmly by the hand and then turned to me. His hair was fair and his eyes were so blue that I could hardly believe they were real. There was a touch of weakness in his face, or it might have been the traces of a childhood illness. It had left his mouth too wide and not quite under control, but it was not obvious and to me it was oddly touching.

"And this?" he asked, a particularly charming smile breaking up his face. By contrast Gideon's quick frown seemed all the sterner.

"Miss Susan King," he introduced us briefly.

"In what capacity?"

I laughed, and the American laughed with me at his own question.

"Cereals—maize mostly, I expect, but I'm hoping for a bit of wheat as well."

"I daresay we can oblige you there. Irrigation and beat-up machinery is my speciality."

I could have hugged him, he was so normal and nice. He bent over and picked up my bags which had now been cleared and started to move off with them to the waiting taxi.

"We must get together," he told me lightly. "Two innocents abroad like us should deal famously together."

"I'm sure we shall!" I agreed, quite as enthusiastic as he.

He grinned. "Sticky journey out?" he enquired.

"Not so much that as a sticky arrival," I replied dryly.

Joseph Groton was immediately sympathetic. He too had obviously suffered from Gideon Wait and he was glad to have a fellow-sufferer, somebody he could grumble with, without it meaning too much, but as a safety valve for good of one's temper.

"It'll be swell having you about!" he said. "What's the kid like?"

I looked back at Camilla with a certain pleasure.

"I like her," I said simply.

"That's good enough for me!" said Joseph. He swung the luggage on to the back of the taxi and went back inside for the next lot. When he came back, he had Camilla eagerly dancing beside him.

"Have you ever been so hot in your life?" she demanded of me. "When is the monsoon expected? Or isn't it? This isn't normal, by any chance, is it?"

"It depends on the time of year," her brother informed her. "It's cooler at the village."

"We're a good bit higher than Delhi," Joseph added by way of explanation.

"And when do we get there?" Camilla demanded. She was tired and like the rest of us, except for her brother, was suffering badly from the unaccustomed and oppressive heat.

"We're stopping the night in Delhi," Gideon announced.

Joseph looked at his superior in surprise.

"Oh, but surely, sir—"

"Delhi!" Gideon snapped.

Camilla and I hurried into the taxi, trying to make ourselves as insignificant as possible.

"Gideon's feeling the heat too," Camilla confided in my ear as we settled down.

"Nonsense!" I retorted with some asperity. "Look at that beautiful creaseless shirt and then look at our dresses!"

Camilla giggled. "He *has* been stroking your fur the wrong way! I'll tell him to tread more carefully!"

"You'll do nothing of the sort!" I told her awfully. She giggled again. "We'll see!"

"Camilla," I begged desperately, "please don't say one word to him. I'll never forgive you if you so much as remind him that I exist!"

Her dark eyes mocked me, and it was with difficulty that I remembered that she was only seventeen.

"Now I wonder what that means?" she said.

Fortunately I didn't have to make any comment, helpful or otherwise, because at that moment the men squashed themselves in on top of us and the taxi made off, with a curious limping motion, towards the road to Delhi. I had never been so close to Gideon before and the experience was a curiously unnerving one. His flesh was as hard as the unpadded sides of the taxi and there was little to choose as to which was doing the more damage to my own more sensitive frame.

The road from Palam Airport ran through miles of deserted land. I craned my neck to try and see the state of the soil, but all I could see was empty country, lying idle, with the occasional tomb dotted about and here and there an obviously new housing development, with that unsettled look of new housing developments the whole world over.

Then we were in New Delhi itself, a large, sprawling garden city, with lots of trees and large flower gardens and, apparently, not very many people at all.

"Disappointed?" Gideon asked me. His mouth was so close to my ear that I jumped despite myself.

"I can't see very much of it," I answered.

He leaned back obligingly and pointed out the main sights to me.

"That's the Prime Minister's house."

I peered round him in time to see the white stuccoed house with its guards in white and crimson with terrific highly starched turbans.

"Where are all the people?" I asked aloud, and then wished I hadn't, it sounded so silly and naïve.

He smiled and his face lost all trace of its former hostility.

"It surprised me at first too," he admitted. "Actually most of the people are in Old Delhi, but Indian crowds are always so silent as almost not to be there at all. I've seen several millions crowding on to the banks of the river on a holy day and there's hardly been a sound out of them."

I felt a tingling sensation of excitement at the picture his words conjured up, but I had no time to day dream then, for the taxi arrived at the hotel where we were staying the night and we drew up with a flourish, the doors flew open and suddenly we were free of the pressure of each other's body and were standing on the burning pavement outside the imposing Victorian entrance to the hotel. A bearer stepped forward with incomparable dignity and signalled to a lesser being to take in the luggage.

"Sahib Wait, you are expected, sir," he greeted us. "And all your party," he added expansively.

We were led gently towards the reception desk and then were taken up by yet more bearers to our rooms in a very grand procession. It appeared that each of us had been allotted a separate room that looked out on to the same terrace where we could all meet for breakfast. Camilla, highly delighted with her new surroundings, ran out to see how much she could see of the city and was pleased to discover that she could look out into the yard of an older and completely Indian house opposite. There a couple of hens scratched in the dust and the children played complicated games, one of which looked remarkably like hopscotch.

"I can almost believe we're here," Camilla sighed with satisfaction.

Her brother grinned.

"We'll go across into Old Delhi and then you'll completely believe it!" he told her.

"Is it terribly old?" she asked him, her eyes round with excitement.

"Well, no, I suppose not," he admitted. "There have been nine Delhis within historical memory, which is one of the reasons one can spend so much time getting from one place to another. New Delhi was built by the

British, Old Delhi by a Moslem overlord, and the rest
are mainly of archaeological interest only."

Camilla eyed him uncertainly. "You planned this
deliberately, didn't you? So that we should see it?"

Gideon shrugged his shoulders. "There won't be much
time once we get down to work," he explained. "I'm
afraid it may be dull for you?"

But Camilla shook her head, her eyes glowing.

"Never!" she averred. "I'm completely happy to be
here."

He smiled at her with real affection.

"Good," he said.

I moved away from them and went into my own
room. It was large and spacious and I was secretly
rather impressed that it should have been allotted to
me. The bed was enormous, a relic from a previous age,
elaborately carved with trumpeting elephants. Over it
hung a mosquito net, tied in a neat knot to keep it out
of the way. On the floor were flung several Indian
rugs and a number of rickety tables with collapsible
legs. I fingered them experimentally, admiring the heavy
brass tops and especially the one made of copper instead, that glowed almost pink in the dim light. Evening
was approaching.

From the window I could see the city spread out
before me, with its wide streets and the pleasant flower
gardens left behind by the British. Once again I
marvelled at how few people there were about and
wondered where they were all hiding themselves. A
young woman dressed in the Punjabi pyjama trousers,
now worn very tight to be in the height of fashion,
moved slowly past on a bicycle. I leaned out a little
farther to see her go, wondering if she were a common
sight or one of the few emancipated women who went
about on their own.

As I turned away from the window there was a sharp
rap at the door. I went over to it and opened it carefully. Joseph Groton grinned cheerfully at me.

"I thought I'd come along and get to know you," he began. "May I come in?"

I stood back to let him enter, a shade doubtful as to whether it was a very good idea to have him in my room.

"Where are the others?" I asked.

He strode over to the window and peered down into the street.

"I suggested they should go off on their own and see some of the sights. Camilla has never had much time with her brother before." He glanced at me over his shoulder. "Do you mind?"

I shook my head, still a little wary.

"Why should I?" I asked abruptly. "It's none of my business."

He swung round on his heel.

"What a prickly creature you are! You wouldn't be averse to making it your business, would you?"

I frowned at him. "I have always found it best," I said coldly, "to leave members of any family alone together."

To my surprise he laughed.

"My, my, what virtue!" he mocked. "Actually the reason I told you was so that you would understand how it is that your evening entertainment rests in my capable hands—"

"You don't have to put yourself out for me, Mr. Groton," I said.

His eyes narrowed with temper. "What's the matter with you? Are you always like this? Or did someone slap you when you expected a kiss?"

I flushed. His words were nearer the truth than I liked.

"I'm sorry. I suppose I'm tired after all that travelling."

He was easily placated. His features relaxed and his weak mouth wobbled into a smile.

"It doesn't matter," he assured me. "I've been looking forward to showing you around ever since I first saw you. And please, it isn't Mr. Groton, it's just plain Joe as far as you're concerned."

He was very sweet, I thought.

"My name is Susan," I told him. "Most people call me Suki, though."

"Okay, Suki!" He extended his right hand and we solemnly shook hands.

"Hullo, Joe," I replied.

He was very easy to be with. From one of his pockets he produced one of those neat guides that Americans always seem to have, packed with facts written in an easy-to-read style. He leafed through it with deep concentration until he came to the section he wanted.

"Ah, Delhi," he muttered. "We have quite an evening in front of us. I think we'd better get a taxi and go over to Old Delhi first. Will that suit you?"

I abandoned, quite easily, my previous idea of an early night and time to get used to the idea that it was really I who had flown all this way and had alighted in this mysterious sub-continent. It would be much more fun to go with Joe.

"Do you ever get indigestion?" I asked him conversationally as we waited on the steps of the hotel for the magnificent bearer to get us a taxi.

"Sometimes," he admitted. "Why?"

I grinned at him, for the first time feeling quite at home.

"Because I'm an expert at dealing with it," I told him.

Old Delhi was a match for my dreams. The ancient Mogul mosques bore witness to a foreign creed, but it was by no means the only one. The Jains, who refuse to kill any living creature, had a bird hospital beside their temple and, it seemed to me, there were a hundred more, all equally colourful and quite unlike what I was accustomed to. The people too were truly of the East. The raucous traffic strove with a thousand bicycles, the walking skeletons of the holy cows, and the Indian conviction that he would be better off in the middle of the road no matter what the hazards involved. The rickshaws, pulled along by hungry-looking individuals on bicycles, wove in and out of the high-powered cars with a breathless unconcern for life and limb. Cars there were by the hundred, but the Indian heart and mind was still with the ox cart and a more sober pace of living. Speed and death merely gave a tang to the endless excitement of living.

We stopped and watched a pavement barber shaving his customer from top to toe. His tools seemed primitive in the extreme, but his fingers were deft and his patter a source of high amusement to those around him. Both he and his victim squatted in the gutter, in a position that came as naturally to them as standing does to us. If I had tried it, I should have been crippled in a matter of minutes, and that as much as anything else made me appreciate the agility of all their movements.

A cloud of yellowish smoke clung over the city in drifts. It had an evil smell and at each street corner seemed to accost us anew. It was only when I saw a small child lighting a small brazier on the pavement and feeding it carefully with dried cow-dung that I realised that most of the people who lived in the city had no houses to go to. They lived, all of them, on the pavement itself, eating and sleeping, playing and working on the same small patch of ground. Some of them had found shelter in some of the shacks that filled the few spaces between the houses that belonged to the richer members of the community. There was no privacy for anyone, but the families seemed to survive, the younger looking after the youngest with loving hands while the parents looked on with a justified pride.

The whole of life pulsated on those streets. Vendors sold their goods, money-lenders and barbers carried out their several services, tailors sewed their goods, using their toes like monkeys to turn the handles of the battered Singer sewing machines that must first have been used in another era. Saris, brilliantly coloured, were laid out to dry. And there was the movement and enthusiasm of a people who were really alive everywhere one looked.

I stopped at a small store that was selling helpings of curry to the passers-by.

"It smells pretty good, don't you think?" I said to Joe.

He cast me a horrified look. "Don't ever eat any!" he warned me. "You'd be in hospital with Delhi belly as quick as knife." I believed him, if a trifle reluctantly, quite sure that my English system would never be able to do efficient battle against that acrid smoke and the dust that was being constantly rearranged by the wind.

"Where can we eat?" I asked him, suddenly extremely hungry. "Do we have to go back to the hotel?"

"I'll take you to my favourite restaurant, if you like," he offered shyly. "It isn't at all grand, but it's the real thing."

I followed him eagerly to his restaurant. Joseph knew Delhi pretty well and he had no hesitation as to which of the narrow streets to take. Most of them I should have been afraid to enter on my own, but his breezy confidence reassured me that we were not trespassing on some illicit underworld and, after a while, I got over my fright and was even able to view some of the desperate beggars with sympathy and interest rather than sheer fright.

The restaurant itself was very small. Somehow between the tables a couple of female dancers gyrated madly to the rhythm of an old man on a flute-like instrument that produced a curious, hypnotic sound. The dancers were fantastic and had muscles in their necks, which they could *move*, that I really don't think even exist in mine. Later on, I tried it out in front of

a looking-glass and retired to bed a casualty, convinced
that I had broken my neck. Actually I had done
nothing of the sort, but it was very sore at the time.

Joseph chose a table in one corner. It was lit by a
single candle, that added romance if not enlightenment
to what we were eating. A singer took the place of the
dancers and a severe-looking waiter with very fine
features and a thin narrow mouth came for our order.
Joseph ordered for both of us.

"It's nice here," he said with pleasure as the waiter
went away. "The food really is Indian, not a con-
glomerate mess mixed with Western cabbage."

I laughed. "I'm expecting great things!" I said.

His hand met mine and took firm possession of it.

"If you could have seen your predecessor—" he began.

It was funny, but I didn't in the least mind flirting
with him.

"I can guess!" I retorted.

"I nearly fell over when I saw the boss had brought
you back with him!" he added, his eyes twinkling.

"I take my work very seriously too," I said.

"Too? You mean you have time for other things as
well?"

I coloured. "Yes, of course," I said. There was a glint
in Joseph's eyes that I didn't quite like. I had to make
it very clear that I had come to work and to wait the
two years for Timothy to get home and I wasn't succeeding very well. "But my work comes first," I added
defensively.

He leaned towards me over the table. I had a mad
anxiety that he was going to burn his tie in the flame
of the single candle.

"You're too good to be true," he said. "Tell me all
about yourself!"

I licked my lips nervously. "There isn't much to tell.
I'd rather hear about you."

His eyes snapped at me. "I'm an American. Isn't
that enough?"

I shook my head. "Tell me about your job here."

He leaned back and relaxed in his chair, a slight smile on his face.

"Certainly not. You'll find out all about that quickly enough. I want you to see me as a man, not as a cog in the great Gideon's machine!"

I was startled into looking at him more closely. His chin quivered slightly and I was reminded again of the basic weakness of his face. But I liked him very much indeed, if only because, in some indescribable way, he reminded me of Timothy.

"I don't think you'll ever be a cog to me," I said gently.

His smile grew warmer. "Is that a promise?"

I nodded my head solemnly. "It's a promise."

His eyes fell to the table. "I can hardly ask fairer than that," he said.

I was a little embarrassed by his seriousness, but at that moment the waiter brought our food and that successfully distracted my attention. It was certainly the most delicious curry I had ever tasted, not as hot as I had expected, but with so many side dishes that I soon lost count. I recognised the desiccated coconut and one or two of the chutneys, and of course the sliced bananas, but the rest I had never seen before and I was anxious to taste the lot.

"Shall we have some wine to go with it?" Joe asked.

I hesitated, wondering about the price. I had been told that it was impossible to have anything alcoholic in Delhi without paying a great deal of money and I was really wondering if Joseph could afford to throw his money away so recklessly.

"No, I won't," I said carefully.

"Oh, come on! One bottle won't break the bank!" He gave the order to the waiter and then sat back looking very pleased with himself. "It will be the first seal on our friendship," he added.

"The first?"

He grinned. "Why, yes, I have plans for the second too!"

I blushed, beginning to think that I was rapidly getting out of my depth. A more normal topic of conversation was more to my taste, and so it was with determination that I brought the subject firmly back to wheat.

"What sort of crops can I expect?" I began cheerfully.

But Joseph refused to be drawn.

"It depends on which crops you are referring to," he answered lightly. "If you're referring to wheat, or sugar, or even rice, you can expect practically no return at all. But if you're referring to *other* crops——"

"What other crops, Joe?" I asked innocently.

"Oh, lies, dirt and disease." He winked at me. "Or friends and neighbours, or even people to love——"

My head lifted sharply.

"I haven't time for things like that!" I said sharply.

"Now, Suki," he reproved me, "you just said you had time for other things besides your work!"

"Not those other things!" I said stiffly.

But he only laughed.

"But you forget," he reminded me, "we've set a seal on our friendship. And if that can be broken, here's another bond more difficult for you to forget." He leaned over the table and caught up both my hands in his, kissing me lightly on the lips.

It was unfortunate that at that moment Gideon and Camilla came into the restaurant. I snatched my hands away from Joseph, but it was too late. A single glance was enough to tell that Gideon had seen the whole incident. I greeted him and his sister with flaming cheeks, doubly annoyed with myself. It was not only that I felt that I had somehow failed Timothy, it was more that I had hoped to give Gideon a quite different impression.

CHAPTER THREE

IT was still very early when Camilla crept into my room to see if I was awake. She padded over to the shuttered windows and pushed them open to let in the first grey light of the day.

"Gideon has gone to pick up the new jeep," she told her. "We're all expected to be ready by the time he comes back."

I turned over and squinted at her against the light.

"What time is it?" I asked.

"It's nearly six," she said.

I turned back on to my side and thought about it. It was the middle of the night!

"What time will he be back?"

Camilla shrugged her shoulders. "Goodness knows! He *says* the garage is only just round the corner, but he's been gone a little while now. You'd better get up and pack your things otherwise he'll start making rude remarks about the way you spend your evenings!"

I frowned. "Actually I don't," I said sourly. "Joseph—" I hesitated. "I think he was trying to be kind," I ended with a rush.

Camilla chuckled.

"I can imagine!" she agreed enthusiastically. "Poor Joseph! If this place is anything like he described it to me yesterday, you must have come like a gift from the gods to him. I can't think why you're even hesitating about him. *I* think he's awfully nice!"

"Yes," I said, "I suppose he is. I don't want to be precipitated into anything, though. He's in such a hurry!"

Camilla gazed at me solemnly.

36

"What are you afraid of?" she asked me. "What Gideon thinks of you?"

I shook my head, hoping that she would not detect the lie that was implicit in my response. I didn't *want* to care what Gideon thought, but that was something a little different, as I knew quite well.

"I must get up," I said instead.

She blinked at me, still serious.

"How old do you think Joe is?" she asked.

I swung my legs on to the floor and stood up, pattering over to the window to have a look at the day for myself. Now that I knew where to look, I could see again the yellow smoke of the cow-dung fires and, thicker still, the fires of the funerals that were taking place along the banks of the river. Life and death intermingled throughout the city and both were casually accepted by the citizens as something unremarkable and every day.

"Does it matter?" I replied to Camilla's question.

"Of course it does! I reckon he's about ten years older than I am, and I think that's about right between a man and a woman, don't you?"

"Possibly," I agreed.

"Humph," said Camilla. "Does that mean you have him all staked out for yourself?"

"Well, he certainly isn't ten years older than I am!" I reminded her.

"No-o," she admitted uncertainly. "But you're not *old*, and he is interested. In fact you might say you had a head start with him!"

I went into the small bathroom which was attached to the room and began to dress, leaving the door open so that I could still hear Camilla.

"One could, if it were a race," I said mildly.

She chuckled, a soft, very feminine noise in her throat.

"Not a race," she contradicted me, "a fight to the finish!"

I hesitated in my dressing, wondering if she meant what she said. But Camilla was still very young and apt to wring the last bit of drama out of any remark. I finished dressing as quickly as I could and gathered up my night clothes to pack them away in my suitcase. Camilla was sitting on the end of my bed, her hair flowing free and a young and rather touching expression on her face. She looked up at me and her face fell into a genuine grin.

"I suppose you're cross with me for challenging your interest?" she said.

It was my turn to laugh.

"Good heavens, no! Joe Groton is nothing to me!"

Camilla was satisfied.

"No," she said thoughtfully. "I dare say Gideon is much more your cup of tea. The trouble is he never sees anyone as a woman. My sister is always complaining about it. You see the truth is that we're all dying to marry him off!"

"Oh, indeed!" I retorted. "Well, there's not the slightest chance of your marrying him off to me, young lady! He's a great deal too confident and full of himself to appeal to my sort of person."

Camilla turned on me, angry at any breath of criticism of her brother.

"What a *smug* thing to say!" she stormed.

I sighed, acknowledging the truth of that. It was the way I had been brought up, I thought, sensibly and without much humour.

"Exactly! And your brother may be many things, but he certainly isn't smug!"

Camilla giggled. "He says he thinks you're a very cautious young woman," she told me. It was getting up so early, I know, but I could have sat down and cried.

It was a peculiar experience, having breakfast in the ornate and gigantic restaurant of the hotel. Two bearers, in braided scarlet coats and with stifly starched turbans, served us an incongruously English breakfast of eggs and bacon followed by toast and marmalade. Both Joseph and Camilla tucked in with concentrated pleasure. I myself thought it was rather hot for such a large meal and I was beginning to wonder what had happened to Gideon and the jeep.

He arrived, hot and more than a little irritable, just as we were finishing the last of the coffee.

"Are you all ready?" he asked.

"Of course we are!" his sister answered him. "Where on earth have you been?"

He sat down at the empty place at the table and nodded to the bearers to bring him his food.

"Getting the jeep," he said with tight displeasure. "It was promised for over an hour ago, but owing to some death in the family I had to wait for the funeral party to come back."

I realised that this was only the beginning of the story.

"And then?" I prompted him.

His face relaxed into a smile.

"And then the plugs needed cleaning and they had to send for a mechanic."

"Didn't they have one?" Camilla asked, entering into the spirit of the story.

"It appears not. I did it myself in the end and it's going, so as soon as we're all ready, we should be going."

In actual fact it was another hour before we were all settled in the jeep with our luggage in a pile under our feet. Joe sat in the front beside Gideon and Camilla and I huddled in the back, both of us a trifle anxious that there seemed to be so very little to hold on to. We crawled out of Delhi, dodging the oxen carts and the weaving bicycles, going so slowly that we had almost got used to our exposed position by the time we had reached the outskirts and the open road.

We had not gone very far, however, before my

equanimity was rudely shattered by the sight of several large animals wallowing in a muddy-pond.

"What are those?" I asked Camilla nervously.

Camilla looked behind us at the dusty trail we were leaving across the countryside.

"Where?" she asked vaguely.

"In that muddy puddle." I pointed beside the road.

"That's a tank," Joseph told me.

"The animal?" I was quite prepared to believe him. They looked very large animals to me.

"No, silly, the muddy pools!"

"The animals are water buffalo," Gideon supplied. "They're quite harmless. Do you want to stop and take a look?" He drew up at the side of the road and helped Camilla and me down into the dust, leading the way towards the nearest tank, and there they were, a whole herd of them, slopping about in the evil-coloured water. They were large animals with black and dark brown hides and they spent hours in the water, standing in as deep water as they were able, their big horns about the only thing to show where they were. And they were not alone in the water. A few naked children played in one corner, chasing each other in and out of the water. Women, too, were taking the opportunity to wash both their clothes and themselves, though how they managed to get anything cleaner in the liquid mud I couldn't imagine.

We climbed back into the jeep and sped on along the endless road, through a dozen small and very poor villages and on to our own. I tried to see as much as I could of the various crops as we went along. Sugar cane grew here and there, looking very tired and undernourished. I longed to stop and take a look at it, but that was to come when we came to our own experimental fields and could see better what would have to be done.

The sun grew hotter and hotter, until the sky was like burning pewter and the hot, dry wind blew up the dust into our faces and dried our skins and made us long for some cool shade and the splash of running water. After a while Joseph took over the wheel from Gideon, driving with a hare-brained desperation that ate up the miles but left us more exhausted than ever.

At last the heat of the day departed and it was evening.

"Not much farther now!" Gideon said cheerfully.

I tried to smile at him, but the dust had mixed with my perspiration, leaving a tight mask across my face. I rubbed my cheeks with my fingers and they came away red with the same dust.

"Cheer up," he said. "It'll wash off easily enough. Besides, it's rather fetching!"

"Nonsense!" I said roughly.

He exchanged a humorous glance with Camilla and I wished desperately that I had said nothing at all, though why I should care so much I couldn't imagine. I had come to work and to fill in two years—nothing more than that.

So I was stiff and rather wretched when we came to the village. Camilla waved to the children who came rushing out to greet us, but I was too busy looking at the extraordinary buildings, many of them plastered with the ubiquitous cow-dung, and the small central shrine around which the women were gathered, seeking the favours of the little stone figure in their midst, representing which god of the Hindu pantheon I did not know.

The jeep pulled up outside a fair-sized bungalow which had a large verandah going right round it.

"This is the central house of the Station," Joseph told me. "Gideon and I sleep here and the laboratory and the records are kept at the back. You and Camilla are going to sleep somewhere else eventually, but come in meanwhile and we'll raise the cook to get us something to eat."

We accepted the offer gratefully. Enormous fans in

every room moved lazily, keeping the air comparatively cool, and it was bliss just to stand beneath one of them and feel the cold current on my face and hands.

"*Memsahib*," said a small, soft voice at my elbow. I glanced down to see the most beautiful little creature smiling gently up at me. It was impossible to tell her age, but the liquid brown eyes held an age of wisdom that contrasted vividly with the youthful firmness of her flesh. She was dressed in a vivid orange sari that was edged with shocking pink and silver that somehow didn't clash but was merely provocative to the eye. With infinite grace she put her palms together and raised them in front of her face in the time-honoured Indian greeting. Her eyes lit up with laughter as I clumsily returned the greeting.

"You have driven a long way?" she asked. "You will need a bath and many clean clothes. It is so hot at this time of year."

The idea of a bath was sheer bliss.

"Is it really possible to have a bath?" I asked her.

The fragile little woman bowed gracefully.

"It will be my pleasure to serve you while you are here," she said in her soft voice. "My name is Lakshmi."

"Lakshmi? The goddess of happiness?" I was proud to be able to show off my meagre knowledge of her religion.

She laughed and smiled.

"She has a little to do with prosperity also," she added. "If you will follow me I shall prepare your bath."

We went out of the main room with its formal chairs and beautiful rugs on the polished floor to explore the rest of the house. One or two pictures, faded photographs for the most part, hung on the walls of the various rooms, decorated with coloured pieces of paper. Closer examination gave no clue as to whom the photographs were of, but they were obviously highly valued by someone in the house.

The plan of the rooms was simple. Somewhere in the centre was the kitchen, a small hole where the cook managed superbly with a small brazier and a few unlikely pots. He squatted on the floor and ground his spices on a flat stone amidst a clutter of utensils. Out of the chaos somehow emerged several meals a day, all immaculately served. It was a constant source of wonder to all of us.

The bedrooms were spartan, furnished only with a single bed, a small table, a chair and a hanging recess hidden by a much faded curtain. There were three of them, all exactly the same. It was easy to recognise Gideon's. Immaculately tidy, it nevertheless betrayed his presence by the titles of the few books and the single strange sculpture that hung on the wall.

It seemed that she was already in the bath and I should second room and into the third. It was exactly the same in every essential as the other, even to the patterns of the dust on the floor.

"You will be comfortable here?" she asked.

I looked at her in surprise.

"I thought—I was told that I was sleeping in another house," I said.

"With the little *memsahib*," she agreed. "This is only for your bath. I will bring it to you now."

With a flash of orange she was gone and I was left alone. Down the corridor I could hear Camilla's cheerful laughter and enough splashing to make me envious. It seemed that she was already in the bath and I should have to wait until she was finished. But two seconds later Lakshmi was back carrying an enormous tin bath of the type I had only ever seen in illustrations of oldfashioned books. She laid it on the floor and filled it from buckets of boiling water.

"Thank you very much," I said, expecting her to go, but she did nothing of the sort. Gently she helped me into the bath and cupping her hands together poured the water over me.

"This is from the Ganges. This is from the Jumna." And so on, naming the Indian rivers one by one, the holy rivers of India. It was an attractive custom, but one which is dying out, she told me, half shamefaced. She had been brought up by her grandmother, she told me, and had learned the custom from her.

It was very pleasant soaking in the hot water. By contrast the air seemed quite cool and by the time I had dried myself and dressed I felt quite fresh and anxious to begin at once by seeing where I was going to work and with whom.

Camilla was still soaking in her bath when I went past Gideon's room and so only the two men were on the verandah as I went out. They both stood up to greet me, their cane chairs creaking comfortably.

"Sit down and I'll get you a drink," Joe said immediately.

I frowned at him. "I—I don't think I will," I said shyly.

"Okay," he agreed easily. "On your head be it."

I sat uneasily on the only vacant chair and watched the two men as they joked with each other, tacitly consenting to let me alone until I should proffer a remark of my own. I hunted through my mind for something interesting to say and came up with precisely nothing.

"The *panchayat* is coming up later to discuss the water supply," Joseph told Gideon over his shoulder, helping himself to another drink.

Gideon grinned. "Sheer curiosity!" he laughed. "They want to see the girls!"

Joseph looked straight at me. "This one will keep them in order," he teased me.

I could feel Gideon's eyes burning into my turned-away face.

"The *panchayat* are the village elders," he drawled.

I turned to look at him. "H-how many of them are there?"

"A round dozen. Someone has to represent each of the many and varied interests in the village."

I began to suspect he was teasing me. "And they are?"

He considered for a moment. "Caste," he began, "and sub-castes, and the landowners and the land-hungry, those who want to build a dam for irrigation purposes and those who don't, and so on."

The very idea of having to deal with such a committee appalled me.

"How—how madly democratic!" I said faintly.

Gideon's eyes twinkled appreciatively.

"There's hope for you yet," he said.

But nothing he had said prepared me for the reality of the meeting. One by one the old men trooped on to the verandah, raised their hands in greeting and sat down with their legs knotted before them on the floor.

"Are we ready?" Gideon asked. He looked very strong and inflexible as he towered above them on his chair. One of the old men smiled at him sheepishly.

"The *Swami* is not yet come," he said smoothly.

Gideon frowned. "He does know we are meeting?"

The same old man answered, "Of course."

Camilla, with her hair done up on top of her head and her neck still wet from her bath, came sailing out of Gideon's room and came to join us on the verandah. Her eyebrows rose spectacularly when she saw the assembled party, but although she was so much younger she was much more self-possessed than I could ever hope to be.

"Good evening," she greeted them with a dazzling smile.

The old men rose in a single wave of movement.

"How pleasurable to make your acquaintance," said their spokesman, and the others nodded emphatically round the circle.

"How lovely to see you all!" Camilla responded cheerfully. She clasped her hands together in inspiration. "Is there any lemonade?" she asked Gideon.

It was Joseph who went to the kitchen and came back with a tray of ice-cold bottles and a bundle of straws. The liquids came in the brightest colours of green and raspberry, orange and the deep brown of Coca-Cola. The old men sucked contentedly at their straws and then, suddenly, a young man with wild matted hair and an orange robe that barely covered his nakedness walked in. Gideon greeted him with evident pleasure, and I offered him a bright green bottle which he gravely rejected.

"Though it is good to see such progress and to have all these good men taking refreshments together," he added with a flash in his eyes. "I shall sit here and study the problems we have before us."

He sat down quickly at my feet and bowed slightly to the other men. With his coming everybody had burst into excited chatter, but at his signal there was complete silence again.

"We have come to talk about the well," the spokesman said in his careful English. "We have paid much for this benefit and, as yet, we can get no water there." It was a bare statement of fact, unadorned and uncomplicated.

The *Swami* sat in silence, apparently not listening at all. The others, more confident now the original point had been made, were positively lyrical about their previous expectations from the new water supply and how badly let down they felt. Finally, when the last man had spoken, the *Swami* turned to Gideon.

"Is this true?" he asked quietly.

Gideon nodded.

"As far as it goes. We are waiting for the electricity to be turned on. As it is it has to be manipulated by hand and the women prefer the old tank down by the sugar cane."

"And the electrician?" the *swami* prodded gently.

"Has not been paid," Gideon supplied wryly.

There was an immediate outburst of indignation as

all the old men tried to explain why their particular group in the village was not responsible for this omission. With mounting excitement they told how the electrician had come and had done the work and then had removed the operative fuse until his bill had been paid in full. But how could they pay until they got the water to irrigate their crops?

The *Swami* listened to them all, waiting patiently while the flow of words went over his head and gradually stilled to a whisper.

"Be that as it may," he said calmly, "it is very annoying to be deprived of your water. What remedy do you suggest?"

The silence became uncomfortable.

"I am afraid the research station has already exceeded the amount that was set aside for the project," Gideon said. There was a thread of laughter under his words which surprised me. It was not lost on the old men either.

"It is such a simple dilemma," the *Swami* went on as if no one had spoken. "I shall place my scarf on the floor here in the corner and after everyone has gone doubtless we shall find enough money on it to pay the electrician. Now, let us drink and be merry."

The old men obediently drank up their fizzy drinks and then one by one they departed, gossiping happily among themselves. The *Swami* sat upright, with his back very straight and his neck bent so that he could look at his toes tucked into his groin. To all appearances he was asleep and completely oblivious to his surroundings. I looked at the saintly lines on his face and wondered at his asceticism. He wore the saffron robes of the oriental monk which I knew betokened celibacy and a laying aside of all the pleasures of this world. Later I was to discover that he was the local holy man with a reputation for charity and that he deserved every word of the praise that was constantly sung of him. Now, he merely puzzled me.

"It was kind of you, *Swamiji*, to come to our assistance," Gideon said when we were alone.

The young man looked up and smiled.

"I think we have more than enough to pay our way now," he said with satisfaction. "And it was my pleasure to come."

Gideon grinned. "Perhaps I should don an orange robe like yours?"

But the *Swami* shook his head. "You will want to marry, my friend. You are ever a practical man!"

"And you are not?"

The wild unkempt hair waved in the wind. "I like to think," the Indian retorted in an affected Oxford accent, "that I can keep my feet on the ground and my head in the clouds!"

We all laughed, and quite suddenly, without a word of farewell, he too rose to his feet and sauntered down the steps and was gone without a backward glance. Joe and Camilla fell over each other trying to grab the money and they solemnly began to count it up. Gideon watched them with a superior smile.

"I'm glad you managed to restrain your western greed until after the *Swami* had gone!" he chided them. But they ignored him, their attention entirely engaged by a number of small coins that added together could only have represented a very minute sum.

"Mr. Wait," I said with a certain firmness, "would it be possible to see where I am going to work?"

His eyes met mine with evident reluctance.

"If you really want to," he said indifferently. He swallowed the remainder of his drink with a gulp and stood up. "I may as well show you your quarters at the same time."

We went another way from the corridor that led to the bedrooms and through a central courtyard that was full of the servants' children laughing and talking together, the small looking after the smallest and making sure that they came to no harm.

"Do they know who belongs to which family?" I asked.

He smiled slightly. "I imagine so."

He pushed open a door and led me into a laboratory. It was cluttered up with papers and useless apparatus and it was quite obvious that it was being shared by far too many people already. Gideon frowned at some evil-looking growth on a tray and shoved it out of sight. His own area was the only neat part of the room. His trays were labelled and his paperwork looked to be in some sort of order.

"I was afraid they would have shoved my stuff completely out of sight while I was away," he muttered. "We haven't nearly enough room."

"No," I agreed, "I can see that."

"In fact," he added, "you will be the final straw!"

I blushed and bit my lip.

"Perhaps I can work in my bedroom," I suggested stiffly.

He put his two hands on my shoulders and turned me to face him.

"Why are you so touchy?" he asked me.

The strength of his fingers burned into my flesh.

"I don't think I am—particularly."

"Oh, come now! Let me disillusion you!" He stared straight into my eyes. "Are you still unhappy?" he demanded.

I shrugged myself free. "Of course not!" I denied in a brittle voice. "I know exactly where I'm going. I'm not in need of anyone's sympathy."

"No?"

"No, certainly not! All I want is to be left alone!"

The warmth and the humour vanished from his eyes.

"In that case you won't take it amiss if I tell you not to tease Joseph, will you? Joseph hasn't got your carefree touch!"

His sarcasm hurt, more than I cared to show

"Why do you think I'd hurt Joseph?" I asked him unhappily.

"He's susceptible. Don't encourage him."

I stood up very straight and glared at him.

"We're friends!"

"Rubbish!" he dismissed me sharply. "Joseph is incapable of being friends with any woman."

I sucked in my cheeks to stop myself from crying. To give my hands something to do I played with the gas tube that fed one of the burners.

"You're not very loyal to him, are you?" I muttered, hoping to hurt him as he had hurt me.

"More loyal than you think! I wasn't thinking about Joseph's well-being when I hired you."

"Too bad!" I stormed at him. "But it doesn't really matter what you say or think. Joe and I have agreed to be friends and I daresay I shall be very much better for him than you think."

Gideon slammed his hand flat down on to the table.

"If by that you mean a repetition of that pretty little scene I witnessed last night, I hardly think so."

I blushed again. I could feel the colour creeping up my neck and cheeks. And then, quite suddenly, I was so blazing angry that I had to hold on to the table to give myself support.

"What a splendidly *scientific* conclusion!" I stormed at him. "Well, as far as I'm concerned you can think exactly what you please!"

His face tightened with temper in his turn.

"Is that so? Then I'll tell you what I think. I think you're on the rebound, young lady, and that one man's attention will do just as well as the next. *And*, what's more, I'll prove it!"

He pulled me towards him and kissed me hard on the lips. The funny thing was that, furious as I was, it wasn't quite so disagreeable as I expected.

CHAPTER FOUR

THUNDER rolled round the skies and was mirrored in my own impotent rage. Gideon let me go and took a step backwards. He looked white and a little less sure of himself.

"Shall we go on with our tour?" I asked him in a funny tight voice I could scarcely recognise as my own.

"I think we'd better join the others," he answered.

Deliberately, I lifted my eyebrows.

"Really? *Afraid*, Mr. Wait?"

His fists clenched as he stared at me.

"Dr. Wait, if you don't mind, when we're working. And no, I am not in the least afraid of you. I have the advantage, you see. I can always sack you!"

The small bit of confidence that temper had given me slowly evaporated before him. I bit my lip, reflecting that he was taking a base and very unfair advantage because his kissing me had had nothing whatever to do with our work. The thunder crashed again overhead and I shivered.

"Is it going to rain?" I asked.

Gideon shook his head. "It's a dry storm. If I turned out the lights you could see the lightning tearing the sky apart. The rain will come later when the monsoons start."

He put his hand up to the switch, but I shook my head in sudden fright.

"I—I think I'd like to go to my room," I said.

He gave me a quick look and I was bitterly self-conscious about my mussed hair and the quivering sensation of tears at the back of my eyes.

"I'll call Lakshmi," he said abruptly and, turning on his heel, he walked out of the laboratory.

Left alone, I could get a much better idea of the work that was being done. A few sickly wheat plants had been pickled in jars and I looked at them with interest. They were a far cry from the wheat I was accustomed to in Europe. I reckoned that the yield from these plants could only be about a half and they were all suffering from diseases that were easily curable. Nearly half of the specimens showed signs of "take-all," a disease of the roots that has practically been mastered in England.

A shadow moved across the jars and I looked up and saw that Lakshmi had joined me in the laboratory.

"Hullo," I said.

She gave me a mildly reproving look, apparently not sure that such a greeting was entirely proper.

"Do you want me to take you across to the other house now?" she asked me.

"If you don't mind," I responded.

She swished her sari more securely around her shoulders and stepped out of the room, half waiting for me to follow her. Another flash of lightning blazed across the heavens and was followed by a heavy roll of thunder. Lakshmi winced and then smiled.

"I am afraid of thunder," she admitted softly. "It is better when it rains, but these dry storms only make me think that the gods must be angry."

I thought I could see what she meant. There was something eerie and supernatural about the white light and the noise and no resulting rain.

"I'm a bit afraid too," I said. "We have nothing like this in England."

She gave me a glance of concealed scorn.

"In England life is very much easier," she said calmly, and led the way through the house and out across the back verandah.

The very air was tense and electric with the storm. I could feel it prickling on my skin and I hesitated to walk across the open space, but Lakshmi went daintily before me picking her way over the rough ground, and I thought that I could not be less brave than such a tiny, delicate creature. But I was glad when we reached the safety of the second bungalow, much smaller than the main building and built on a similar, though simplified, pattern of a whole lot of rooms all looking out into the central area where the life of the family was mainly lived.

Lakshmi entered one of the small, practically bare rooms and went over to the window, flinging open the shutters.

"If you need anything, you have only to ask me for it," she said almost apologetically. I looked round the room with a feeling of dismay. It was so foreign to my previous ideas. A single bed, low and threaded with string instead of springs, stood in one corner against the wall. There was no table beside the bed and very little in the way of bedding. Apart from the bed there was only a desk and a home-made wooden chair with one leg at least an inch shorter than the other three. An old frayed rug had been spread across the floor, somehow accentuating the poverty of the rest of the furnishings.

"Where do I keep my clothes?" I asked, trying to keep my outraged shock out of my voice.

Lakshmi smiled. She went over to one of the walls and pressed it with both hands. To my surprise it opened at her touch and revealed a spacious cupboard that was almost a dressing-room.

"Everything is kept here," she said. "It is too hot to have much in the room with you."

I was touched by her unspoken sympathy.

"I'm afraid many things will be strange to me," I murmured.

A fresh outbreak of thunder almost brought the house down about our ears. Lakshmi stood, slight but foursquare, and still smiling.

"I think you will very soon grow accustomed to our ways," she said.

A lot of things were strange that evening. The storm rolled away to the distant hills and left the air as hot and as sultry as ever. Occasionally one could see a servant sweeping, but the dust never disappeared. It covered everything, white and sandy, making the same inevitable patterns in the corners of the rooms. And then, later, there were the suicide squads of insects trying to kill themselves in the oil lamps on the verandah. A servant came to let down the netting in an attempt to keep them out, but they came through every crack and cranny, in all shapes and sizes, some of them huge and looking like inhabitants of another planet, some of them small but equally frenzied in their attempts to reach the light.

"Now I know I'm home," Gideon said, surveying a particularly nasty specimen crawling up his trouser leg. How peculiar, I thought, that he should think of this strange and rather frightening place as home. I looked from him to Camilla, who had found a moth and was studying the pleasing sable of the fur on its wings with every sign of delight. It must run in the family, I thought, and crept farther away into the shadows to be by myself. I felt very remote from them all and rather lonely. When I thought of Timothy I wanted to cry, and yet when I tried to make myself remember his face I could only recall the most obvious facets as if he had been no more than a stranger.

Joseph had gone to his room much earlier and later on I had heard the sound of the jeep going out and had presumed that he had gone out. I didn't like to ask where he had gone, but I found that I missed him. Once or twice I surreptitiously looked at my watch and wondered when we were going to eat. A variety of highly spiced smells had been coming from the kitchen for hours, but one glance inside had told me why it took so long for the meal to be forthcoming. The cook had to grind every spice by hand to make his curry, which he did with tremendous care, making a fresh lot every time.

"Hungry?" Camilla asked me.

I flushed, aware that I had been looking at my watch yet again.

"I think I must be," I answered her.

Gideon looked up from his drink and smiled. "We have to wait for Joe to get back," he said calmly.

Camilla was prepared to argue the point.

"Joseph wouldn't mind if we started without him," she said impulsively.

"No, but his companion would!" her brother retorted.

I pricked up my ears, astonished. "Is there anyone else here?" I asked.

Gideon's smile became mysterious and quite aggressively masculine.

"Not here. Joe has gone to fetch her for dinner. She comes round quite a lot when we're here." His eyes sparkled. "She's very pretty and a gentle little thing. You're both to be kind to her!"

Camilla gave him a very sisterly look.

"You've been holding out on us!" she accused him. "Who is this mysterious woman? Are you in love with her?"

Gideon gave her a lazy slap. "That's none of your business!" he reproved her. "Her name is Julie Burnett and she lives here. Her father stayed on after Independence. He has a bungalow in the next village— he retired there. I'm afraid it makes for a rather dull life for Julie."

"How old is she?" Camilla demanded.

He looked at me consideringly. "I suppose she's about the same age as Miss King."

Camilla frowned. "I should think she's older than that! Suki's father hasn't retired!"

It was my turn to frown. I was not enjoying having the two of them discussing me while I was sitting there, especially not as something told me that in Gideon's eyes at least I was only a pale shadow of this Julie, who was quite obviously the love of his life.

"The Burnetts didn't get married until quite late. Julie is their only child and the apple of their eye."

Camilla made an unpleasing face.

"I can imagine!" she said.

Gideon's face lost its good humour.

"Camilla! Julie is a very attractive person, and if you can't be civil you can go to your room." And then, most unfairly, he turned on me. "And that goes for you too, young woman!"

Just what I should have answered, I hate to think, but at that moment we could hear the jeep approaching and, a second later, Joseph's exuberant laugh as he brought Julie round the house to join us.

It is difficult to describe the impact Julie had on Camilla and me. She was very small and dainty and walked with a bouncy little step that somehow made sure that everyone was looking at her. She was something to look at too! Her hair was rinsed the palest mauve and apparently her clothes and her make-up had been chosen to match. With difficulty, I stopped myself staring at her and went through the movements of greeting her. If *this* was what Gideon wanted, I thought, no wonder he disapproved so heartily of me!

"How do you do, Miss Burnett," I said bravely.

Her grey eyes rested gently on mine. It was impossible to tell what she was thinking. I watched her closely as she turned away to Camilla and managed, just in time, to stop myself disliking the faintly patronising smile she gave the younger girl. I would not allow myself to make any impulsive judgements. Not yet!

We all sat down in a little semi-circle. Miss Burnett pulled her chair as close to Gideon's as she could manage, and I was oddly comforted when Joseph did the same to mine, with a proprietorial air that at another time would have amused me.

"Settled in?" he asked me.

I nodded my head, pleased by the attention he was paying me. I felt *at home* with Joseph.

"More or less." I grinned suddenly. "I haven't tried the bed yet!"

He gave me a sympathetic look, joining in my laughter.

"When I first came I didn't get a night's sleep in a week! But after a while you begin to appreciate the simplicity of the arrangements in this dreadful heat!"

To my surprise Miss Burnett giggled and joined in the conversation.

"I suppose they've given you one of the Indian beds, a *charpoy*! But you don't have to be so uncomfortable. You can get anything you want in Delhi."

Gideon hooted with laughter.

"At a price! And who wants an interior sprung mattress here?"

But Julie Burnett was not so easily put off.

"*My* family all have proper beds. We wouldn't have anything else."

Camilla and I exchanged glances. Nothing could have reconciled us to our string beds more quickly. It was with difficulty I refrained from laughing. Poor Gideon! Whatever he felt about Julie Burnett himself, his family were all going to hate her! She was not at all their style. I thought back to the house in Putney and his sister's family and the children and, frankly, I couldn't see Julie there at all!

But Gideon couldn't leave well alone.

"Why ever not?" he demanded.

Julie looked decidedly sulky. "Someone has to keep up some kind of standards," she muttered. "None of you make any attempt to do so here! Poor Daddy thinks it's dreadful the way you dress and—and everything. He doesn't really approve of my coming here at all, so there!"

Gideon immediately looked contrite.

"I know," he said heavily. "It's difficult for you living here, without many friends of your own kind."

Julie patted her pale mauve hair with a certain sensual pleasure.

"Now, now, Gideon darling, you needn't look so down in the dumps! I shan't stop coming, no matter what anybody says! As I keep telling myself, someone has to keep you up to the mark, and I don't suppose you would eat properly or anything unless I saw that you did!"

I couldn't bring myself to look at either of them in case I should discover that they were both as embarrassed as I was. But Gideon, when he spoke, sounded nonchalant and almost indecently cheerful.

"Good for you! Let's go and eat, shall we?"

We sat at a long table, on hand-made cane seats that were cooler than anything else would have been. Camilla was annoyed because, while her brother sat at the top of the table, Julie had placed herself firmly at the foot with her usual giggle.

"I always act as hostess for Gideon whenever I come," she had explained to us all at large.

It didn't worry me a great deal, because I was sitting next to Joseph and he was a much easier companion than any of the others.

A moth, larger than any I had seen before, swooped over the table towards Julie. She screamed very daintily and Gideon leapt to his feet and flicked his napkin at the winging creature. The attraction of Julie's hair was too much for it, though, and it settled on the top of her head, waving its antennae menacingly at the rest of us.

"Keep quite still!" Gideon commanded.

But Julie was quite beyond doing anything of the sort. With frenzied movements she tore at her hair.

sobbing audibly as she gulped rather than breathed. Camilla watched her with indecent enjoyment.

"I should have thought," she said in clear, young tones, "that someone so accustomed to India would have been able to deal with a *moth* !"

"Shut up !" Gideon said tautly.

"Well, really, it's quite harmless !" Camilla argued placidly. "Why don't you scoop it into a glass?"

Gideon looked decidedly put out.

"I don't want to spoil Julie's hair arrangement," he said helplessly.

Camilla looked hard and long at them both. "Could you?" she asked lazily.

It is difficult to say who was the angrier, Gideon or Julie.

"I hate your sister !" the girl sobbed hysterically.

"I'm not surprised !" Gideon agreed grimly. And then, quite suddenly, his lips began to quiver and his laughter rang through the house.

"I'll never forgive you ! Never. Never !" Julie stormed at him. "I'll never forgive any of you !"

I felt decidedly sorry for her. Because I was not in the least afraid of flying things myself, I picked the moth up by the tips of its wings and put it firmly outside the shutters.

"You ought to do something to keep them out," I said to Gideon.

He gave me a look which I thought held admiration.

"Are you always so calm and collected?" he asked me softly.

I shook my head, suddenly tongue-tied. He was very charming when he wanted to be—too charming for my comfort !

"Well, we can all be grateful to you this evening at least," he went on. Deftly, he encouraged Julie back into her seat, smoothing down her hair with gentle but efficient fingers. "Let's get on with dinner, shall we?"

We all sat down again, trying not to notice the red,

swollen eyes of Julie Burnett, looking reproachfully round the table. Only Gideon paid her much attention, listening to her weak jokes and jollying her along with such blatant flattery that my respect for him zoomed down to zero again.

"Is she here often?" I asked Joseph in an undertone. For some reason he coloured slightly.

"A fair amount. We provide most of the entertainment hereabouts." He smiled quickly as if he were afraid of what I was thinking. "She won't bother you much," he added. "She only ever has time for Gideon."

Camilla frowned at him across the table and he blushed to the ears, realising that the whole table had probably heard what he had said.

"What I mean is that you'll be pretty busy," he went on desperately.

"And me?" Camilla asked him coolly.

"Ssh!" said Joseph.

Julie Burnett became suddenly aware that something was going on. She stopped fussing at her face and hair and glared at Camilla.

"Gideon always said you were a spoilt brat, but I don't care what you say. A silly little chit of a girl doesn't bother me!"

I glanced sharply at Gideon.

"That's enough," he snapped. "This is meant to be a pleasant occasion. I guess the heat is getting the better of us. Camilla, ring the bell and clear the soup plates. Perhaps the heat of Gobal's curry will cool us all down."

The curry was very hot and the meat was tough. I ate it slowly, washing it down with some of the buttermilk that was on the table. Unexpectedly, I liked it, for I should never have tried it on its own. I tried as much as possible to ignore everybody else at the table, talking only to Joe, and that worked very well because the others fell into an uneasy silence and then began to speak of the local crops and village affairs until even

Camilla joined in with a sudden spurt of interest in the condition of the local soil.

But I was glad when the meal was over and Gideon and Julie went back to the verandah to sit by the spirit lights in the black darkness and to gossip about the days they had spent apart. Joseph excused himself by saying he had to work and I dragged Camilla off to our own house while the going was good.

"I suppose they're all right alone," she said wistfully.

"They'll manage," I agreed heartlessly.

"You mean *she* will! Suki, we'll have to do something about that blue-haired doll."

"But what?" I asked.

Camilla put on a scheming expression and I knew she was beginning to enjoy herself.

"We'll think of something," she said sweetly.

Lakshmi had turned down my bed. Apart from the cover there were two natural-coloured cotton sheets stretched over the thin khaki mattress. There was no bedside light, only a single unshaded electric bulb hanging from the ceiling that buzzed at intervals as the voltage changed. I had been accustomed to some kind of discomfort in my digs, all the time I had been studying. But this, coupled with my weariness of mind and body, was enough to reduce me to tears.

I undressed slowly because I was still unaccustomed to the stuffy heat. The storm had started up again and I could feel its electricity against my skin. In a peculiar way it was exciting and I was sure that sleep would be a long time coming even when I had got into that uncomfortable bed. But I had underrated my tiredness. All I could remember was that the bed was not nearly as bad as I had expected, and then I was asleep, heavily and dreamlessly asleep as only the very tired can be.

When I awoke it was pitch black. I lay on my back and listened to the peculiar sounds of the Indian night.

The curious scratching noise of some insect on the ceiling, the wild howling of some large cat outside the settlement, and a variety of undertones, all so different from the softer nights I was accustomed to at home. I turned my pillow over, looking for coolness, and was surprised to hear the sound of the jeep going towards the main house. As it passed the yellow headlights came flooding through the windows on to my bed and passed on again. I glanced briefly at my watch. It was a little after three o'clock. I supposed bleakly that it was Gideon returning from seeing his girl-friend home. And a fine time of night it was too! I thought crossly, and then berated myself for being narrow-minded. But even so I couldn't believe that he would be really fit to do much work in the morning.

I was awake again at half-past six. The grey light of first dawn was already being broken up by the yellow and orange streaks of the rising sun, a perfect background for the lovely old trees that shaded the settlement of bungalows and a few of the village buildings that were caught up in the research station grounds. I hurried into my clothes and wandered outside to take a look round by myself, before anyone else was up.

The village people were already stirring. I was particularly interested in a small one-storied mud house that clung on to the wall of the research station's kitchen garden. The wall which faced its own small yard was covered with hand-made dung cakes drying in the sun. The woman of the house, bejewelled with bits of gold in her nose and round her ankles, was slapping at a few more cakes with her hands and smacking them on to the wall. It gave the house a very peculiar appearance with a series of hand-prints showing where the dung had been slapped on.

I nodded and smiled, muttering good-morning inadequately. The woman came over to where she could see me better and watched me with intense curiosity as

I walked round the end of the wall so that I could see her house better. We stood in silence, staring at one another. Slowly, she drew her sari up over her head in a gesture that meant very much the same as an English housewife patting at her hair before she answers the door. She continued to stare at me with the same unblinking curiosity that I frankly shared but hadn't quite got her self-confidence to indulge it in quite the same way.

Eventually she beckoned me over, putting out a wondering finger to touch my dress and the cheap costume beads that I wore round my neck. Then suddenly she smiled and giggled shyly as I smiled back. Grasping my wrist, she led me into her tiny domain, showing me the pots that she scoured with sand and calling to her children, who had been playing naked in the yard, to go into the house and put on the ragged shorts which were all they had in the way of clothes. Somehow the woman made me understand that she was in some way related to Lakshmi and that therefore she had heard all about me. It obviously struck her as very funny that a woman should be involved in Gideon *Sahib's* work. I don't think she realised that her own Prime Minister was a woman.

I was fascinated by the varied signs of the life they led in that courtyard. Two small braziers in one corner were obviously what she cooked on, and a string-bed standing on its side by the gate, made me think that they slept outside if at all possible also. The woman touched my sleeve and pointed to the door, and so, for the first time, I set foot in a completely Indian household.

There were only two small, airless rooms inside, windowless and smelling heavily of dung. Most of the walls were of unpainted mud with garish pictures of the Hindu gods pinned up here and there. A few essential household effects, like a mortar and a couple of shallow pans mostly used for making *chapattis*, the

Indian unleavened bread, and some storage jars, completed her few possessions. I congratulated her on them eagerly, all the more so because I was wondering if I could live on such a little.

We came out into the sunlight again and I saw Lakshmi standing in the yard waiting for me. My hostess said something to her and they both smiled at me.

"My sister is honoured by your visit," Lakshmi said softly.

"Your sister? She told me you were related," I replied.

Lakshmi laughed. "She is older than I, and I am not yet married," she told me simply.

I wondered briefly how the younger sister had managed to learn English and to get some kind of an education.

"I have been admiring her home," I said.

Lakshmi nodded. "It is poor, but she is very happy." We said our goodbyes and strolled slowly back to the main bungalow of the research station.

"Did they send you to find me?" I asked Lakshmi anxiously. I glanced at my watch to see what the time was, but it had stopped. With irritation I shook it and it started to tick again.

"The *Sahib* is already up, but the others are still in their beds," she answered calmly. "It was the *Sahib* who wished you to come to breakfast."

Gideon was sitting on the verandah when I joined him. A pile of letters rested on his knee and he was looking at them with a curious expression of displeasure mixed with a reluctance to do anything about them.

"How did you sleep?" he asked me abruptly.

I stood pointedly ignoring the question until he rose to his feet and offered me a chair at the table.

"Dr. Wait, where do you want me to begin?" I enquired coolly. "Do you want me to go straight out into the fields?"

He glared at the letter he had at last opened. a few seconds his eyes met mine.

"Miss King, I have put you in charge of the and maize results. What you do with your time is own affair."

Quite what made me take him to task, I imagine. I opened my mouth and to my dismay question hung on the air.

"Even if I come in at three in the morning?" taunted him.

"I gather you didn't sleep well, Miss King," retorted blandly.

"I happened to see the lights from the jeep, that all," I muttered.

"Just *happened*, Miss King?"

Furious with myself for getting myself into such a position, I bit my lip and tried to look cool, calm and collected.

"I was turning over," I said.

His amusement was very difficult to bear.

"I see."

"I—I'm not used to the heat yet," I added by way of explanation.

"No," he agreed, half laughing. "And it does such terrible things to one's curiosity, doesn't it?"

"I—I suppose it's a long way to Miss Burnett's house. I'm not really interested," I finished loftily.

Gideon grinned at me, thoroughly enjoying my confusion.

"It takes about twenty minutes," he told me confidentially. "But of course it's very romantic driving home in the moonlight."

"It must be!" I said sourly.

He leaned over the table until he was close enou to touch.

"The trouble with you, Suki, is that you're not as prickly as you pretend to be. You're plain jealo

"Nonsense!" I said sharply. "It isn't true!"

CHAPTER FIVE

CAMILLA decided to come with me when I set off to inspect the fields. She couldn't pretend to any interest in either wheat or maize, but she was set on avoiding her brother for the rest of the morning.

"Gideon is different out here," she complained. "He hasn't time to talk or anything."

"He was on holiday in England," I reminded her.

"And Julie is part of his work, I suppose!" she retorted tartly.

I had no answer to that! My own burning feeling of injustice was too much with me for that.

"Perhaps we won't see very much of her," I said hopefully instead.

Camilla snorted sulkily. "Would you care to bet on that?"

I pretended basely that I hadn't heard her. I pulled my white overall out of my suitcase and put it on, thrusting my hands into the starched pockets and wriggling my shoulders to make it more comfortable.

"Good heavens," said Camilla, "you look more like a doctor than an agriculturist."

"A plant doctor," I suggested with a grin.

She smiled back. "Something *very* impressive! I wish Gideon could see you now!"

I glanced at myself in the looking-glass on the wall. To my eyes I looked young and very vulnerable and not very impressive at all.

"I don't suppose he would be taken in by any exterior," I said wearily. "It's the results he will be looking at."

Camilla gave me a worried look.

"But Gideon is always fair!" she exclaimed. "Unless

that mauve witch has put a spell on his judgement as well," she added.

"He's a grown man," I said carelessly. "He wouldn't let anyone interfere with his work."

Camilla looked young and very tragic. "Other men have," she said.

We went out through the laboratory. Gideon was standing by the window studying a stick of sugar-cane. He was plainly surprised to see Camilla, but he said nothing, much to my relief, because Camilla was in a mood to argue whatever he said to her.

"I suppose you know where your fields are?" he asked me.

I shook my head. "I'm on the verge of finding out," I replied cheerfully. "I thought I'd have a look round before I did anything else."

He nodded. "I'll point you in the right direction and then let you find your own way. Has Joe laid on any transport for you?"

"Not that I know of."

He made a quick gesture of disapproval and went to the door.

"Joseph! Have you laid on a jeep for Miss King?"

Joseph appeared in the doorway, a piece of half-eaten toast in one hand.

"Look here," he began, "I haven't even finished breakfast yet!"

"The rest of us have," Gideon informed him coldly. "Go and get a jeep ready now. And *shift* yourself!"

I threw Joseph a quick look of sympathy. He might be slow getting up, but at least *he* hadn't been out until three in the morning.

"And come straight back here," Gideon ordered.

"Yes, sir!" said Joseph.

I grabbed my notebook and prepared to follow him. One glance at Camilla's sulky face was enough to know that her sympathies were all with the young American.

"Come on," I said hastily. "We have a lot to do."

Her eyes flashed, but she said nothing. I grabbed a pen and put it in my pocket, pushing her out of the door before me.

"It isn't fair!" she said under her breath as we walked round to the garage. "What has Joseph done?"

One thing Joseph hadn't done was to get our jeep ready. When we caught up with him he was standing helplessly surveying the vehicle that had been officially designated mine for the next two years.

"Gosh, Suki," he exclaimed, "I'm frightfully sorry. I guess I forgot all about it."

I surveyed the four flat tyres and the generally depressed look of the dusty jeep.

"Can we walk it?" I asked hopefully.

Camilla jumped into the jeep and pressed the starter. There was a soggy squeal, telling that the battery was flat too.

"Surely there must be some way of making it go?" she said.

"None at all," said Gideon's voice from the entrance. He walked forward and glanced at the forgotten jeep. "You'd better take Joseph's while he goes to work on yours."

"But—" the American began.

"But nothing!" Gideon said sharply. "It was your job to get the vehicle ready. Okay, so it's you who has to do without transport today."

"You're not using yours," Joe objected.

"That's beside the point." Gideon handed me a roughly drawn map of the village showing the fields in which I had an interest. "Think you can manage?" he asked with a smile.

I hesitated. I was very much aware of the atmosphere between Camilla and Joseph and the man who was giving all the orders, and yet he had reason, especially if Joseph really was in charge of keeping the vehicles on the road.

"Perhaps Joe could show me the way?" I suggested humbly.

To my surprise he laughed.

"If you want him! But that jeep had better be ready for you tomorrow morning. Did you hear that, Joe?"

Joseph grinned sheepishly. "Right," he said. "I heard."

Joseph drove us straight through the village and out the other side. I got tantalising glimpses of the small industries that went on the dark little shops that lined either side of the road. The oil merchant and his press which was driven by a single bullock that trudged endlessly round and round the home-made mortar. Next door was a bazaar in miniature, a hundred different colours represented by saris, ribbons, shirts, turbans, and a few odd lengths of material spread out across the narrow pavement in the dust. Beyond that was the tailor, working his sewing machine with one foot as he used his hands to guide the material under the needle and, beyond him, the village potter, squatting beside his wheel and making the few simple pots that the local housewives demanded.

Beyond the village the fields began—dry, dusty tracts of ground that grew little and were so badly in need of water that I almost despaired there and then.

"This is your main wheat," Joseph said, nodding with his head towards the driest of all the fields. "Not much hope for that!"

"No," I agreed. "Where's the nearest water?"

Joseph made a face.

"There's a stream over there. In the monsoon it bursts its banks and washes everything away. In the hot weather it just forms tanks for the local buffaloes to wallow in. It's not much help."

I looked at the deep cracks in the dry earth where the wheat was struggling to get a living.

"It might be," I said.

Camilla didn't want to walk across the baked field to have a look at this rather doubtful water supply.

"I'll wait here with Joe," she said prettily. "It's too hot for all of us to drag round."

I expected Joseph to say that he would come with me, but he didn't. He gave Camilla a shy little smile and shrugged his shoulders.

"Whatever the ladies command of me!" he said with mock gallantry.

Somehow I hadn't got the heart to insist that he came with me. I pulled my hat farther over my eyes and went off alone. It was farther than I had thought. The wheat straggled on for several acres, most of it looking little better than the average seeding grass. At intervals I took samples of the earth, sealing them into separate envelopes and marking them so that I should know where they came from. At intervals I pulled up one of the plants and examined the root carefully. Some of them were badly eaten by various pests, a few suffered from root diseases, but the vast majority were dry and brittle from lack of water. I broke a couple of straws and looked at them gloomily. I had a long way to go if I was going to make a go of this thing, and I was beginning to wonder if I had the necessary knowledge and experience even to begin.

The stream when I reached it was so sluggardly that the water hardly moved at all. A few buffalo were immersed in their tanks, sharing the brown waters with one of the women from the village who was busy washing both herself and her family's laundry. I waved to her and she waded to the bank to return my greeting more formally.

"*Namaste*," she said.

I placed the palms of my hands together. "*Namaste*," I replied.

I sat on the dusty bank and watched the woman as she went back to her work, banging the clothes against a large flat stone that effectually blocked up most of the trickling stream. The water behind built up slowly, very slowly, into a muddy outsize puddle. It was remarkable to me that the clothes should ever get any cleaner, but after a while she was apparently satisfied and laid the garments out in the sun to bleach and to dry.

I bade her a tentative farewell and made my way back across the baked field. I could see Joseph and Camilla sitting in the jeep, sitting side by side, intent on their own conversation. They were in no hurry for me to get back, I thought dryly, and wondered why I should resent the young man's light interest in Gideon's sister. It struck me forcibly that two years was a very long time and I had no security that Timothy would come home to me at the end of them.

By the time I had come up to them they had got out of the jeep and walked the last few yards to meet me.

"This heat!" Camilla exclaimed. "Aren't you completely exhausted?"

I smiled, a little amused by that. It would be a fine thing if I couldn't complete a single day's work, having come all this way!

"It's certainly hot," I agreed.

Joseph flapped his shirt against his chest and grinned at the two of us. "Where now?" he asked.

"The next field," I retorted.

It was much the same story wherever we went. Neglect and drought vied with each other to be the main cause of the poverty of the crops. On the whole I thought drought won. Even such water as there was was not reaching the plants, and here lay my first and most immediate problem. Gideon hadn't told me, but I thought that our funds were probably pretty tight. It was possible that the government helped a little, but the sort of irrigation scheme I had in mind was expensive even by European standards. It was not the sort of thing that small villages like this one were likely to ever get.

Joseph and I tried to rally the thoroughly bored Camilla on our way home.

"You can come and help me fix up the other jeep after lunch," Joseph offered, very much in the manner of a small boy offering to share one of his best toys.

"I shall be lying flat on my back trying to get cool," Camilla retorted. She saw Joseph's face fall and took pity on him. "Perhaps I'll come along after I've had a long cold shower," she compromised.

Joseph flushed. "You don't have to," he said awkwardly. He glanced at me and then suddenly began to laugh. "Suki, honey, your face hasn't half caught the sun!"

He was right, of course. By the time we got back to the main bungalow it was already burning. One glance in the mirror was enough to tell me that by tomorrow I would be lucky if it wasn't peeling. And at the back of my mind I discovered that it wasn't the thought of the inevitable pain that disturbed me most, it was that Gideon would see me at such a disadvantage, and that was a particularly humiliating thought. I didn't want to give a rap about what *Gideon* thought. What Timothy thought, thousands of miles away in America, would surely always be much more important.

Gideon was out at lunchtime. We all of us wondered where he was, but there was nobody to ask. We sat on the verandah and played with a vegetable curry and the inevitable buttermilk that goes to make up the diet of the Hindu. The food was very good, but it was too hot to eat, and I made my escape as soon as I could and took my samples to the laboratory to test the content of the soils while I had the place to myself. It was work that I enjoyed. I had always enjoyed mixing concoctions and making magic potions that resulted in accurate information. I was at home in the laboratory; I felt confident and sure of myself, and the rest of the world was very far away.

It was almost dark by the time I had finished. I heard

the jeep come in and I listened for Gideon's footsteps to come towards the laboratory, but they stopped at his bedroom. I was bitterly disappointed. I sat in the gloom and waited longer, but there were no further sounds, and after a while I began to see how silly I was being. With a sigh I began to put my things away, neatly coding my results in the appropriate files that I had already prepared. When I had finished I walked through the house and paused for a second on the verandah. There were monkeys chattering in the trees, pulling at the leaves and chasing each other up and down the branches, jumping down on to the ground and up again, like so many bad-tempered children.

"Had a busy day?" Gideon asked from behind me.

I turned swiftly. Gideon's hair was wet from the shower. It stood on end, gleaming in the last of the light.

"Yes," I answered. "It is a depressing prospect without more water."

"Oh, I shouldn't say that," he said cheerfully. "There's a long way to go, I know, but the soil is pretty good."

"I've just analysed various samples of it," I said dryly.

"And?"

"And the sooner we get some nitrogen into it the better!" I said grimly.

"Look, I know that soil—" he began.

"Do you?" I asked him tartly.

"Perhaps you'd better let me have your findings," he sighed. He looked rather depressed and I wondered again what he had been doing all day. "Though where I'm going to conjure the stuff up from I don't know!"

"It's the lack of water that I'm really worried about," I insisted.

Gideon grunted. The water from his hair was dripping down the back of his neck and he pulled out a handkerchief to dry himself. Across one corner was a smear of pale mauve lipstick. My sympathy for him died dramatically.

"The new well will help," he said.

I gave him a scornful look. "It might," I agreed, "if anyone was around to work it!"

"Is that intended as a reference to me?" he asked stiffly.

I shrugged my shoulders. "If the cap fits—" I drawled.

To my surprise he looked amused.

"I'll tell you when it does," he said.

Somehow, I thought dismally, he had managed to get the last word again. But it wasn't that which hurt. It was that small smear of pale mauve lipstick that was the unkindest cut of all.

In the morning my jeep was ready for me and so I was independent of what anyone else was doing. I liked it that way. I spent most of my mornings out on the field and my afternoons checking my findings and working in the laboratory. Gideon managed to procure various chemicals, but it continued to be the lack of water that worried me most. When I was not worrying about my work, I worried about myself. I could feel myself growing daily tighter and more intense, but I didn't feel that I could relax with anyone at all any longer. Whenever I did I got hurt too badly, or so it seemed to me.

I was sitting at the bench in the laboratory when the *Swami* came in. He came and went as he pleased, his saffron robes flapping in the dusty breeze. Everybody respected him and was pleased to see him, including myself. I soon got used to his shock of wild hair and his ability to remove himself from any conversation by the simple expedient of staring into space with his soft, enormous eyes completely vacant of any expression. He came and glanced over my shoulder at what I was doing.

"You work very hard, Miss King!"

I struggled with myself not to notice the matted hair so near to mine, or the strong smell of spicy foods that came from his skin.

"What I need most of all is water," I told him bitterly.

The *Swami* nodded gravely.

"We must all concentrate on that," he agreed. It was funny to hear his pure Oxford accent coming out of such a frame.

I looked up at him beseechingly. "I suppose you wouldn't like to work your magic on the *panchayat* to make them pay for some kind of an irrigation scheme?" I begged him.

He shook his head with finality.

"A village this size doesn't have that kind of money, Miss King. You would need a miracle worker for that sort of thing."

I sighed. "Would it really cost so much?"

"In money? Perhaps not. But so much more than we could afford."

Reluctantly I was forced to agree with him. In a land where a roof over one's head spelt riches and the possession of a bed and a chair something to be talked about and envied, where could the money come from for such a project?

"I suppose so. But, *Swamiji*, you do see the necessity for more water, don't you?"

He looked at me, his eyes doleful.

"I am not a fool, Miss King," he said.

"No," I said, a doubtful note creeping in despite my very best efforts. "But there must be some way of doing something!"

He laughed. "If you can think of it, Miss King, then I will be happy to follow *your* lead," he said, thus neatly returning the problem to me.

"Well, I shall have to think of something!" I agreed. "That is, if we are to grow wheat here at all."

He said nothing more and after a while I returned to

my work, though I wasn't nearly as able as he at with-drawing from my surroundings. After a while he shoved a bony finger towards my figures and said :

"It wasn't really to discuss your work that I came to see you."

I threw him an enquiring glance.

"No?"

"I thought you would like to accompany me through the village to see the new pump."

I was highly gratified. For a moment I tried not to show it, but the smile of pleasure spread across my face just the same.

"Is it really working?" I asked.

He nodded. "So they tell me."

I threw down my pen and stood up immediately. I had been astonished and appalled by the delay in getting the well into action. The electrician had had to come from afar and not even the thought of getting his money had been able to tempt him to hurry back to the village.

We walked through the village as if we owned it. The *Swami* strode on ahead, his robes rippling in the wind; I followed a pace behind, anxious as always to see every-thing that was going on all round me. The *Swami* must have been more observant than he looked because he stopped suddenly in the middle of the street and I practically walked into his back. As always in the presence of a foreigner a knot of begging children had gathered, more curious than determined. The boldest of them touched my skirts, while the others put their hands over their faces and peered through their fingers.

"It will be well when my people learn to be a little less materialistic," the *Swami* said sternly.

I laughed. "You want too much !" I teased him, a little shocked by my own audacity. "They have to eat !"

"But not by begging."

My lips twitched. I could hardly help it.

"No, but by giving me water for my wheat!" I retorted.

He shook his head at me.

"You must ask Mr. Wait for that."

I sighed. "I suppose so," I said.

There were surprisingly few people at the well. I thought I recognised most of the women drawing water. They were very graceful, filling their pots and carrying them off to their various houses on their heads, but it was plain that the vast majority of them were still using the water from the buffalo tanks. We stood and watched for a while, trying to fight down a feeling of disappointment that the whole village was not making use of it as we had hoped.

I went forward to the edge of the well and peered down into its depths. There was very little to see, for the new electrical machinery took up most of the space and one could only glimpse the water below.

"It is working well now," the *Swami* told me, not without pride. "At first it was difficult to get it going because none of us knew how to prime it."

I giggled, remembering similar pumps in the country where we had spent our school holidays when I was a child. I put my two hands on the edge of the well wall and exchanged smiles with one of the youngest housewives I had ever seen. Aged no more than twelve, she nevertheless had the proud bearing of one who was sure of her own status. For an instant I thought by her looks that she too might have been a relative of Lakshmi's, but as soon as she had filled her earthenware pot and raised it to her head, the likeness went and she wandered away down the street and was lost in the crowd.

I had been so busy watching the first girl, I didn't see the second until she was right on top of me. She had none of the confidence of the first, but was quite scared to actually take the water from the well. I stood up straight to help her, but other hands were there before mine. To my surprise, I recognised them to be Gideon's.

"Will you get me water to drink?" he asked her.

She was plainly overcome by such a request, but his smile reassured her and it was obvious that she didn't like to refuse his request.

"The water is tasteless after the other," she told him shyly.

"It is clean," he replied. "The other water holds many illnesses inside it. This will keep your children well and strong."

She licked her lips doubtfully.

"My husband will say my cooking is not as good as his mother's," she went on.

Gideon laughed. "All husbands say that anyway!" he teased her. "You try it and see if he doesn't compliment you on your new skill."

She was overcome with feminine amusement at the very idea, but she dipped her pot into the water and offered it to Gideon so that he could drink, which he did with such a natural air that the other women gained in confidence and came closer to see the fun. Gideon was completely at home with them. He was never familiar, but within seconds they all felt at ease with him and he had forgotten that he was a stranger bringing strange ideas into their lives.

The *Swami* watched paternally from the edge of the ring of women.

"I shall leave you in his capable hands," he said to me in amused tones. "He is already managing to do what I came for."

"To win their confidence?" I asked him.

The *Swami* nodded solemnly. "Exactly that."

He was gone almost before I was aware. I saw the flash of his saffron robe as he disappeared down the street and I wondered again at the Indian's ability to merge into his surroundings so successfully as to be practically invisible.

Gideon, suddenly bored with his admiring audience, came away from the well and joined me on the edge of the throng.

"Working hard?" he asked me wryly.

I kept my head with determination.

"There's blight on some of your potatoes," I told him, figuring that the best form of defence was to attack.

He smiled quite affably.

"I know. I'm dealing with it tomorrow." His grin grew bigger. "Afraid it will spread on to your fields?" he prodded me.

"Of course," I retorted. "My wheat is parched, but it is at least *clean*!"

He was still amused, and I wondered what had put him into such a good temper.

"Famous last words!" he said.

But I refused to be drawn.

"I haven't got enough water on those fields to feed a bug!" I turned to face him. "Dr. Wait—"

His smile died.

"Suki, don't dare to mention water to me again!" he reproved me. "I haven't the time or the inclination to go into it now."

But when would he have? I wondered. I allowed my eyes to drop from his face, but not before I had noted the signs of fatigue in the corners of his eyes and the faint shadows that sketched his muscles in more clearly than usual. If he had been home at a reasonable time, I thought, he would be more able to do his work. I suppose my thoughts must have been mirrored on my face, because he grasped me firmly by the hand and pulled me down the street.

"You and I," he said, "are going to the *pan* seller and there we'll sit in the shade and regain a sense of proportion!"

I didn't know what a *pan* seller was, but I followed him willingly enough. I liked being with him, liked it more than was good for me. It was because I liked his society so much that I fought shy of it, sensing its dangers and rather enjoying the sensation.

The *pan* vendor had chosen an ideal spot beside a bank. Gideon and I sat on the red dust and watched him beside us. He squatted by the side of the road, his little cabinet beside him and with a potful of leaves covered with water. When Gideon nodded to him, he carefully prepared a leaf for each of us, covering it with various spices from the little drawers in the cabinet, lime and cutch, cardamon seeds and cloves and the inevitable shred of finely beaten silver which, for some reason, all Indians seem to think essential to their good health.

Gideon received the first leaf and popped it whole into his mouth, chewing it cautiously at first and then with obvious pleasure. I could smell the spices as he ate them and, when he had finished, his mouth was as red as if he had swallowed a dollop of red ink. I was not at all sure at first that I liked the taste when I got my own leaf, but the taste was so clean and fresh that I was sorry when I had reduced it to pulp and there was nothing left to wonder over.

"Now, about this water," Gideon began.

I waited for him to go on, but he was lost in thought.

"Well?" I prompted him.

"We'll have to make better use of the monsoons," he said. "The streams fill up then—too much so."

I thought of the muddy trickle that ran beside the wheat field I had looked at first of all.

"I shall build a dam myself," I announced. The spices from the *pan* had practically blown the top of my head off and I felt quite capable of doing anything. "It isn't impossible," I went on, "the water is *there*!"

Gideon gave me a long, hard look.

"All right," he said slowly. "See what you can do, but don't come crying to me if it doesn't work."

My back stiffened with sheer temper.

"I shouldn't dream of it!" I told him coldly.

CHAPTER SIX

JULIE BURNETT invited Gideon and Camilla to spend Sunday with her parents. For some reason Joseph and I were not included in the invitation. I don't think either of us minded much, but Camilla took immediate offence at the whole arrangement. After the incident of the moth, no one had expected her to become exactly friendly with the other girl, but we couldn't help feeling that a certain tolerance was desirable.

"I won't go!" she told her brother.

Gideon barely looked up from the paper he was reading.

"Don't be ridiculous," he said.

Camilla, who was not often or easily put out, completely lost her temper.

"Nothing will induce me to go! Why should I? Besides, why can't she ask all of us? She's a horrible snob and I won't have anything to do with her!"

Things were not made better by Gideon leaving the room as if he had not even heard her.

"Would you go?" Camilla demanded. "Imagine his *liking* such a person!" A terrible thought struck her. "Suki, you don't suppose he would actually *marry* her, do you? Because no one else in the family will survive the shock!"

"Oh, Camilla!" I protested, because I didn't like the idea of Gideon married to Julie myself. "I imagine your brother will make up his own mind when it comes to marriage."

"Possibly," she agreed tearfully. "But I couldn't live in the same household with her."

I sighed. It wasn't my place, I supposed, to break it to her that she might not be wanted by her brother once he had married. I half-thought that I might try and prepare the ground, but the very idea of Julie living on various research stations round the world was so ridiculous that I hardly knew where to start. It was funny that we should all think of her as such a social creature when really she lived right at the back of beyond and probably had had as few parties and outings in her life as I had.

"I don't suppose Gideon is really serious about her," I said pacifically. "He has to be polite and so do the rest of us."

Camilla stared at me, wide-eyed.

"You mean I shall have to go on Sunday?"

I nodded regretfully, but Camilla became quite cheerful about it.

"Okay, I'll go. It will be quite interesting to see what sort of people managed to produce a freak like Julie anyway."

I frowned at her, but I had to admit that I would have been interested myself. It was terrible to be so curious and I couldn't help being glad that Gideon didn't know of my interest, for I was quite sure that he would have had no sympathy with my own vivid dislike for the other girl.

I thought Gideon looked grim and strange in a jacket and tie when he got the jeep out on the Sunday. Camilla had excelled herself by producing a filmy nylon dress that clung to her youthful figure and a picture hat that gave her a quaint dignity. It was only when she was stepping up into the jeep that I saw she was also wearing elbow-length gloves and a bracelet which was as valuable as it was ornamental. She caught my eye and grinned.

"Somebody has to keep the flag flying," she said tersely.

"Oh *yes*!" I agreed. I was having difficulty to keep from laughing and I was afraid that Gideon would see. As it was, I thought I caught an answering gleam of laughter in his eyes, but I knew of course that I must have been mistaken. One doesn't stay out until all hours of the night with a girl unless one admires her.

"What are you two going to do with yourselves?" Gideon asked as he started up the engine. For a minute he sounded quite envious of our freedom to do as we wished.

"I'm going to get the dam started," I said.

Joseph stood with his hands on his hips, twisting his belt with his thumbs.

"I guess I'll help," he said indifferently.

Gideon hesitated, looking worried.

"D'you think you can manage on your own?" he asked.

"Why not?" I asked him.

He smiled slightly at my challenging attitude.

"Go carefully," he bade me. "You can't accomplish everything at once."

I hardly listened to him. I certainly didn't think his caution was important. I noticed how easily he slipped the jeep into gear and in a short while they had disappeared in a ball of dust. Poor Camilla, I thought, what a dull day she was going to have. But my own day was full of the most exciting prospects. I turned to Joseph with enthusiasm.

"Will you go and round up the men?" I asked him. "The sooner we begin the better!"

The gentlemen of the *panchayat* stood in a group at the edge of the field looking with distaste at the hardly moving muddy waters of the stream. They did not understand my plans for the dam and they were plainly suspicious that any female should conceive such a plan.

"The water is small and narrow," they argued. "How will you make it more? It will never be enough to water the whole field."

It was difficult to argue in a language with which

they were not very familiar. I found it easier to show them. Accordingly I built a tiny dam across one of the trickles that went to make up the stream. I tried to explain how I should build a tank on either side to take up the water and how I would slowly build the two walls towards each other, with sluice gates in the centre which could be opened during the monsoons to control the floods. The old men watched with interest. They nodded their heads and discussed the plan between themselves. One of them had a son who had travelled right across India to see a similar experiment in another district. It had brought prosperity to the whole area, he reported eagerly, and the other men believed him. They knew how important water was to the crops. They also knew what it was like to live in times of famine and they knew that the research station made this less likely in their own village.

"It would cost very little," I encouraged them.

Two of the very oldest men hitched up their clothing and came and stood beside me in the stream. With eager hands, I described exactly where the dam would be built, splashing around in the water and getting myself thoroughly muddy and wet.

"It would need much labour," the old men said finally.

"There are young men in the village," I replied eagerly. I knew that there would be the difficulty of caste, but I was hoping for the best. I wasn't at all sure what sort of a working force I would get, but I was reasonably sure that I could manage no matter how few they gave me.

"We would have to pay for the sand and the cement?"

I nodded unhappily.

"But the field would repay the expense in a single season," I countered.

The old men scuffed their toes in the muddy waters and thought some more.

"We shall do it," they said at last. "We shall do it if Mr. Wait agrees to the plans. We shall discuss the whole matter with him."

I agreed to this, shaking hands with each of the old men in turn. When they had gone, I found myself alone, still up to the ankles in muddy water and completely content because I knew that somehow I was going to make the wretched field productive.

I was still standing there, gloating, when Joseph came to find me. He could not have been mistaken for anything but an American. He wore his hat at that particular angle and his trousers skin-tight with his shirt hanging out. He sat down on the bank beside the stream and took out his cigarette case. It flashed gold in the sun as he opened it and offered me a cigarette. I accepted one gratefully. American cigarettes were so much bigger and I like their more mild tang when I smoked them.

"Thank you very much," I said.

"How did it go?" he asked.

I sat down beside him, trying in vain not to grin too triumphantly.

"Well, I think. The actual decision is to be referred to Gideon."

"Oh well, that was only to be expected. You don't mind, do you?"

I felt quite breezy with confidence and didn't mind at all.

"Not a rap!" I assured him.

He grinned. "Good for you! I'll be right in there, cheering for you!"

But I wasn't as sure of him as I wanted to be. For all the length of time I had been on my own, making my own friends and answerable to no one, I was strangely ignorant of the ways of men. When I thought about it, there had been only one man whom I had really studied and that was Timothy. The thought of him made me wince, because I wasn't even very sure of him.

"I can manage very well on my own," I said to Joseph.

He wasn't in the least put out.

"Nonsense. You're going to need all the help you can get! Friends on these occasions are half the battle. Didn't you know that?"

"I've heard it," I admitted cautiously. "But how can we be sure of our friends?"

He was hurt. I watched helplessly as he struggled with his feelings. First he was angry and then more chagrined.

"What have I done to offend you?" he asked at last.

I shook my head, searching for some way of easing the wound I had inflicted.

"I wasn't thinking of you in particular," I assured him. "It's more that I never realised how personalities come into this kind of work."

Joseph flashed a look of enquiry at me.

"You can't expect to live in your shell for ever," he said quite gently.

"I suppose not," I agreed abruptly. "But it would be a great deal more comfortable!"

Joseph laughed. He had fully recovered his good humour and was determined to jolly me out of my introspective ways.

"Have you forgotten that we set a seal on our friendship?" he reminded me.

I blushed a little, remembering his kiss.

"No," I said uncertainly. "No, I hadn't forgotten."

"Well then," he began reasonably, "how could you even suppose that I would desert you in any hour of need?"

I thought about it seriously, wondering at my own lack of confidence.

"I'll tell you what it is," I confided in him on a note

of sudden levity, "I have the feeling you're the friend of every girl!"

His mock indignation amused me.

"I might flirt a little—but I never hurt anyone, do I?"

I wriggled my feet in the sun. The mud had baked hard around my toes and it was a pleasant sensation breaking out of the cocoon of sandy clay.

"There's Camilla."

Joseph started guiltily. "You ask an awful lot of a guy!" he expostulated. "Camilla is a pretty little thing!"

"Very pretty!" I agreed lazily.

"But too young for me, of course!"

"Oh yes?" I prompted him.

He put his hand on his heart. "What do you want, Suki? A full-blown confession about how I cast a glance in her direction?"

I shook my head. "Camilla isn't my business. You're not either, come to that!"

"But supposing she were?" he prompted me. He rolled over on to his side and gazed at me with innocent eyes. "Supposing we both were, what then?"

I smiled lazily at him.

"I'd warn you off, I suppose."

"Because Camilla is only seventeen?"

"I suppose so."

He plucked an ear of corn and tickled my nose with it.

"And would that be your only reason?" he asked me.

I sneezed. I had never played this sort of game before and I was surprised to find that I was enjoying it.

"I don't know. It might be."

He reached over and kissed my cheek. "I consider myself duly warned off." He kissed me again. "Especially when there's such tempting bait so close to hand!"

"Joseph Groton."

He looked very innocent, young and all-American.

"Are you warning me off again?" he asked with an injured air.

He was terribly attractive and I didn't think of Timothy at all.

"I'm not warning you at all," I said.

"Lakshmi!"

The Indian girl came running. She had a new sari on of peacock blue edged with white and silver. She looked as bright and as quick as a kingfisher flashing through sunshine and water.

"My, my!" she exclaimed. "Where have you been, Miss Suki? I'll set the fire and draw you a bath straight away!"

I brushed the red dust off my cheeks and laughed.

"I've been talking to the *panchayat* about building a dam—"

Lakshmi gave me a bright-eyed look.

"Did Mr. Joseph help to persuade them?" she asked. "I am sure he would have liked to have done!"

"He came when it was all over," I replied repressively.

"And very welcome, I'm sure," she said in much the same tones that I could remember my mother using.

I met her teasing, feminine eyes as calmly as I could.

"Perhaps," I admitted.

The bath was glorious. I lay in the hot water, sniffing delicately at the tinny smell of the bath. It was surprisingly comfortable and I began to think that before the days of bathrooms and glamorous tiles, people might have had some quite good ideas about comfort after all.

I was just drying myself when the telephone sounded shrilly in the hall. Annoyed, I waited for someone else to answer it. What could it have been but someone from the main house wondering where I was? But Lakshmi was afraid of the telephone and she ignored the sharp ringing of the bell until I could bear it no longer and, pulling my towel around me, I pattered out into the corridor and picked up the receiver.

"Yes, what is it?" I asked testily.

There was a gulping noise at the other end.

"What's the matter?" I demanded.

"There's been an accident!"

I pulled myself together and clasped my towel more tightly around me.

"Where? What happened?"

"This is Julie speaking—"

"Oh, really?" Despite myself my voice was tinged with ice. "Are you hurt?"

"No, no! It isn't me. Though I must say I was very nearly badly hurt as well. It was so careless and unnecessary. Gideon ought to have known better!"

At the mention of his name I felt cold and all the more impatient for her to tell me exactly what had happened.

"Julie, has anything happened to Gideon?"

She gave a quick, breathless laugh, from nerves rather than from amusement.

"That's what I'm trying to tell you. Gideon would insist on playing polo and I told him that the horses were wild—and—and it slipped."

I had a terrible vision of Gideon lying, twisted, on the ground while Julie wrung her mauve-tipped fingers on the side-lines.

"The pony slipped?" I prompted her hollowly.

"Yes," she gulped. "It was awful! I cried and cried."

That I could imagine.

"And Gideon?" I asked dryly.

"He's broken a leg. And, really it's most peculiar, he wants you to come out immediately and drive him home."

"Me or Joseph?" I asked.

"He said you," Julie answered in the same bewildered tones. "It isn't at all necessary. I *told* him I would drive him and Camilla home and stay on and nurse him, but he said I would be more useful calming my parents. They're terribly upset, naturally."

"Naturally," I agreed. "I'll come straight away."

I could imagine the scene as I put down the receiver. Camilla sulky and unresponsive, the parents annoyed that such a thing should have happened in their perfectly run Indian retreat, and Gideon, impatient with pain, shouting orders at everyone. Julie wouldn't like that at all! It was the centre of the stage for her, or nothing at all, and I couldn't help being sneakily pleased that she had been deprived of her star billing for a while. If it hadn't meant Gideon being hurt, I should have cheered!

My mood of elation died speedily when I tried to get the jeep out of the garage. Joseph had put it away for me and apparently he hadn't noticed that one of the rear tyres was completely flat. I looked at it with dismay. The familiar pricking sensation of heat on the back of my neck was already with me after my bath and the accompanying feeling of helplessness made positive action doubly difficult. I tried to find Joe, but he had already gone out again. Thoroughly dispirited, I went back to the garage and started to change the wheel myself.

I had got the jack working and two of the nuts loosened when one of the workers came in for some of the chemical solution Gideon was using on his potato fields. He took the wrench out of my hands and finished the job for me, talking all the while as he did so.

"Going far, *memsahib*? There is no other spare tyre for you to take with you."

He was quite right, but I really couldn't bother about that at that moment. I thanked him warmly for his trouble and jumped up into the driving seat. I had only the vaguest idea of where I was going, but I was reasonably sure that I could find the way if I started off right, and as there were only two roads leading out of the village, I could hardly go wrong.

The road went through trees full of chattering monkeys. It was difficult to get away from animal life in India. People, monkeys, cattle, birds and insects jostled one another for existence. Even in the most unlikely corners a lizard would suddenly come to life to impale a fly on its tongue. Snakes came and went, seeking peace and solitude and sometimes food, and terrifying everyone they met. Normally I rather liked to see this teeming life all round me, but that day the monkeys became almost intolerable, throwing twigs and stones at the jeep and swinging down towards me out of the trees until I really began to believe they were going to leap in with me.

I was not yet frightened, but unconsciously I hurried more and more until I was going so fast that it was scarcely safe on the inadequate double track. I forced myself to slow down, but then the monkeys came again, and by this time I was really rattled and kept telling myself it was only because I was alone.

I took the most used track when I came to the first fork. The jeep crashed over a half-concealed stone and the engine faltered. So concerned was I to keep the thing on the road that I failed to catch the faltering spark and the engine died completely. Swearing under my breath, I pulled in as far as I could and tried to get started again. The monkeys came closer and closer, inquisitively watching my every movement. One of them, braver than the rest, jumped down on the bonnet and pulled a face at me. I was really scared then. They were so incredibly human in their movements, like so many evil old men, jeering at my vain efforts and the squealing self-starter.

I remembered having been told that monkeys were sacred in India because Hanuman, a demi-god and an ape, had formed an alliance with the god Rama and had helped him to find Sita, Rama's wife, after she had been raped by the demon king of Ceylon. Looking at this particularly large specimen on the bonnet, I began to think that their help had been overrated, or certainly man's gratitude had been, for these animals were completely unafraid of me and came closer and closer, teasing me with bony fingers and chattering movements of aggression.

It was a great relief when the engine suddenly sprang into life. I blew the horn and started off down the road again, scattering the monkeys as I went. I was so hot now that the perspiration ran down my face and tasted salt on my lips. It was farther than I had thought and I was beginning to wonder if I had come the right way. I came to a small village and made enquiries from the only inhabitant I could find. The directions he gave me were vague in the extreme, but I gathered that I was on the right road.

When I finally reached the entrance there was no mistaking it. Two enormous lions, made in concrete, marked the gates, towering over the sign that said this was the Burnett residence. Beyond this imposing beginning was an avenue of trees, now badly neglected, but nevertheless still handsome. I set the jeep up the rough drive and rumbled over the pitted surface towards what had once been a quietly tasteful and spacious house. Now it was painted in a violent pink with the windows and doors picked out in a vivid blue. The roof was overgrown with a mossy plant and a general air of neglect brooded over the place. It was not at all the sort of home that I would have thought would have appealed to Gideon, and I wondered what had first drawn him there.

Halfway up the drive a man leaped out from behind a tree and waved me down. I came to a halt beside him and he jumped up beside me with a flurry of words.

"Missee come very quickly. *Sahib* Wait very sick man. Better you take him home. This house not welcome to a sick man. One sick man more than enough, don't you say? Missee Julie wait for you on verandah. The *memsahib* gone to bed."

"Oh?" I said weakly. "Really?"

"Not a good day for anyone," the Indian went on with complete satisfaction. "Very sad!"

"Do you know where Dr. Wait is?" I asked him.

"But of course. That is why I wait for you to come, to show you the way. I am the most completely reliable servant. You will see."

I began to think that he might be as he directed me to drive round the house and to park the car in the shade of a large tree to keep it cool.

"I take you straight away to *Sahib* Wait," he told me. "We shall not wait for niceties of various greetings as they are taking too much time. Come with me immediately."

He led the way, his bare feet completely silent on the stone floor of the verandah, and took me through a door that was swathed with mosquito netting to keep out the flies and other lesser animal life. It was dark inside and very cool after the heat outside and I stood still for an instant just enjoying the contrast. The Indian beckoned me onwards and opened a door into a darkened bedroom.

"The *Sahib* is in here," he said.

It was a minute or so before I could see much beyond the general shapes of the furniture. I went over towards the bed as quietly as possible in case Gideon was sleeping.

"Hullo, Suki."

I jumped, terribly relieved that he should sound so very much himself.

"Oh, Gideon!" I gulped.

He chuckled, and I was very conscious that I had used his Christian name and not his title.

"Why did you come?" he asked. "I thought it would be Joseph."

I hesitated.

"I answered the telephone. Julie said you wanted me

to come." I couldn't have sounded very sure of myself because he hastened to reassure me.

"A much prettier chauffeur, anyway."

I could see him more clearly now. He looked as hale and hearty as ever and not in the least in need of my sympathy.

"Julie said you were hurt!" I exclaimed.

He made a face at me. "So I am! I rather think I've broken my leg. Damned pony rolled on it."

I tried to look sympathetic, but my curiosity overcame me.

"What on earth were you doing playing polo?" I asked.

He grinned. "I do play, you know," he said. "And anyway, the old man likes a game. I'd forgotten all the same," he went on dryly, "that he couldn't bear to lose. I shot the second goal for my side and then bang, wallop, and this!"

"What *do* you mean?"

"I mean that he tripped up my mount!" he said bitterly. "If I could prove it—but I can't, so what the hell?"

"But that's dreadful!" I exclaimed, shocked. "And where's Camilla?"

"In a state," her brother replied. "I told her to go off by herself and calm off until the doctor came."

I gave him a furious look.

"How could you?" I demanded hotly. "You know she didn't want to come in the first place! I'll go and look for her!"

A strong hand shot out from the bedclothes and grabbed me round the wrist.

"Oh no, you won't! I know exactly how she's feeling, but she has to learn to get on with the rough as well as the smooth. Julie spent all day being nice to her, but she couldn't come out of her sulks sufficiently to see it!"

I tried to imagine Julie being nice to anyone and failed miserably.

"I don't think she will ever like her much," I put in.

"That's beside the point!" Gideon snapped back. "She doesn't like Julie's parents either! Nor do I, for that matter, but Julie is the one who has to live with them day in and day out, and I admire the way she does it, without a word of complaint. She has courage, that girl!"

I felt quite as sulky as Camilla must have done.

"And where is she?" I asked.

Gideon leaned back and closed his eyes. Accustomed now to the dim light, I could see the lines of pain etched in around his eyes and the paleness of his cheeks.

"She's getting a doctor."

There seemed to be nothing to do but wait and so I sat down gingerly on the edge of a chair and looked about me. There was no mistaking the fact that the owners of the house had lived in India for a long time. The only table was mounted on an elephant's foot and various trophies hung round the walls, trailing ribbons that were faded and dirty, relics of an era that had completely disappeared. A tiger's skin lay on the floor, the head realistically growling in my direction.

"I suppose someone shot it?" I said with distaste.

Gideon laughed weakly.

"Mr. Burnett, no doubt! What an impossible girl you are!"

We sat in silence after that, waiting for someone to come and restore our spirits. Gideon was more and more obviously in pain and I getting more and more worried about him. But when Julie and the doctor came it was almost an anticlimax. Julie came running into the room, the tears sparkling in the corners of her eyes and her pale mauve hair prettily ruffled by the wind.

"Gideon, he says you'll have to go to the hospital for an X-ray. What shall we do?"

Gideon opened his eyes and looked at her.

"Nonsense! Tell him to come and set it here and then I can go home."

Julie caught his hand in both hers. "You're so terribly brave!" she sobbed.

I looked at the two of them with growing disgust.

"I suppose you want to limp for the rest of your life!" I said with some asperity. "Of course you'll still go to the hospital. Where is the doctor?"

A small Indian doctor, dressed in a Congress cap and very little else, approached bowing from the doorway where he had been standing.

"The gentleman is in much pain," he said softly. "Perhaps it would be better if the ladies left until I have made him more comfortable."

Gideon laughed shortly. "Perhaps you'd better!" he said.

Julie walked tearfully towards the door with me following, a pace or two behind. I felt sorry for her, knowing the ravages tears can make and that she would care, but, oddly, she cried as easily as a child. The tears welled into her eyes and down her cheeks without a single sign of reddened lids and the headache that I am left with. With her it was actually pretty.

"Poor Gideon!" I said with a sympathetic smile.

The tears came harder and she frowned at me.

"Yes," she said. "But do you know that child actually said it was all our fault! As if it wasn't bad enough for poor, darling Papa. I shall never invite *her* here again!"

Which was just as well, I felt, as I very much doubted whether Camilla would have come.

CHAPTER SEVEN

CAMILLA was decidedly sulky, but she cheered up a little when she saw me.

"How's Gideon?" she asked immediately, and I couldn't help feeling that they had been rather cruel to take her away from him.

"He's all right!" I told her. "What did you imagine? He's more impatient than hurt!"

"Really?" She took a deep breath of relief. "It was awful!" she added, and shivered at the memory.

Julie rounded on her savagely, her face pinched with temper.

"You keep quiet, miss!" she spat. "We've had enough trouble from you!"

I was startled out of the composure I had assumed for Camilla's benefit.

"What do you mean?" I asked.

"You weren't there!" Julie said nastily.

Camilla went scarlet with rage and so I cut in quickly before she was really rude to her hostess.

"Of course I wasn't there and I'm very glad I wasn't. It was obviously a great shock to you all. May Camilla and I go out into the garden while we wait to find out what the doctor has to say? And then I'll be taking her home—and Gideon too if he's well enough."

Julie recovered herself with difficulty. Her face was still pinched and white round the mouth and her eyes blazed with temper as she looked at me, but her voice was as soft as honey as she answered.

"Of course you want to have a look round," she agreed. "I'll go back to Gideon and see if he wants anything."

I nodded my head and she went tripping out of the

room, her soft hair bouncing with her steps. Camilla contained herself with difficulty until she had gone and then she burst into tears. There was nothing attractive about her crying and she made things worse by rubbing at her eyes with her knuckles like a child.

"It was awful!" she said again. "Suki, they tripped him because he scored a goal. I *saw* them!"

"But it was only a game," I said easily. "Who was playing?"

"That's what was so ridiculous!" she exclaimed tearfully. "There weren't enough people to play a proper game of polo and so they were really just playing about. Mr. Burnett was on one side, with two of the servants to help him, and Gideon and the other two were playing against them. They set up a couple of makeshift goals, and it was terrific fun at first—all the time Mr. Burnett was winning. He shot a goal almost immediately and we all clapped like anything and he was terribly pleased. But then Gideon whacked two into the other goal almost before he could turn round and he *deliberately* pushed his stick between Gideon's pony's legs. Of course the pony tripped!"

"It could have been accidental," I suggested.

"You wouldn't think so if you'd seen his face!"

I found myself believing her, even though I didn't want to because there was something rather nasty about her story, just as I had thought there was something nasty about the whole house.

"All the same, I think you'd better forget all about it," I warned her.

Camilla gave me a curious look.

"Because you believe me?" she asked.

I hesitated, more than a little embarrassed by the question.

"Hush," I said hastily.

It wasn't any too soon to change the subject because at that moment Julie joined us again, all smiles and without a trace of her former rage.

"How nice it is to see you both enjoying yourselves," she purred. "And I have some good news for you too! The doctor says it's a clean break and he's setting it now, so Gideon won't have to go to hospital."

"Good," said Camilla bluntly, "then we can take him home with us!"

Julie frowned quickly through her smiles.

"Now, now, I know how much you want him with you, dear, but we must consider the patient a little too, mustn't we? He'll be much better off here with us."

Camilla opened her mouth and I knew she was getting ready to argue the point, probably at the top of her voice and with more feeling than would have been proper.

"Of course we shall do whatever is best for him," I agreed warmly.

Camilla gave me a stony glare.

"Traitor!" she whispered under her breath.

I smiled on, until I began to think that my face was setting in a mould and that the strain was beginning to show.

"May we go and talk with him?" I asked politely.

It was easy to see that Julie would have liked to have refused, but as there was no good reason why she should, she nodded briskly and walked quickly off, leaving us to follow.

"You're not going to leave him?" Camilla whispered anxiously in my ear.

"Not if I can help it," I replied grimly. "But Gideon won't do anything on my say-so. He'll make his own decision."

Camilla sighed. "I expect you're right, but it would be *fatal*!" And, even allowing for adolescent exaggeration, I couldn't help wondering if she wasn't right.

Gideon was sitting up against a pile of cushions with his leg smothered in wet plaster and a rather foolish grin on his face.

"Lovely mud pies!" he greeted us cheerfully.

Camilla went quickly over to the bed and took his hand in hers, squeezing it hard.

"You're sure you're all right?" she asked him in a funny, tight voice.

He laughed up at her.

"You worry too much, young lady! Give this muck time to set and I'll be sitting beside you in the jeep while Suki drives us both home."

Camilla swallowed tearfully.

"*She* said you would rather stay here!" she said rebelliously.

"Did she though?" He laughed in the most light-hearted way. "That's no reason to make such a mouthful of the whole thing." He gave me a quick look and seemed to be reassured by what he saw, because he threw the whole conversation into my court by saying: "Aren't relatives the very devil?"

It was the wrong question to ask of me, who had been bereft of relatives for some years now.

"You ought to be glad to have someone to care about you," I reproved him.

He made a face at me. "Is that what your Timothy would have said?"

My sympathy for him died. I was nonplussed as I always was whenever he referred to Timothy. For long stretches I forgot all about Timothy myself and I was both edgy and wary when anyone reminded me of him. I felt somehow that they were calling in question my devotion to him.

"He really *needs* someone to take care of him," I remembered. "I do hope he's eating the right things in America!"

Gideon and Camilla exchanged impatient glances.

"Well, really!" Camilla fired at me crossly. "As if it matters that your Timothy lives on stomach powders! Gideon is really hurt!"

Gideon's raucous laughter did nothing to smooth my decidedly ruffled feathers.

"Don't worry, chicken," he said to his sister, "I'll be coming home with you!"

We both sighed with relief.

"I hope you're going to tell Julie," I said feelingly.

His eyes shone with amusement. "You're quite as bad as Camilla," he teased me. "Seeing bogys where there are none! And making such a fuss about it!"

I would have made some retort that would have put him firmly in his place, only Julie rejoined us at that moment, as sweet as ever and as full of smiles.

"I'm so sorry to have left you on your own," she began with that 'little girl' charm I was beginning to despise. "I just called in to see how Daddy is getting on. It was such a shock to him. He's lying down, poor darling. Mother was too, but now she feels strong enough to see you two girls before you go home. She's in the drawing room. Shall I show you where?"

Camilla looked suddenly defeated.

"It's all right," she muttered, "I can find it." She stood up with a quick coltish movement. "Come on, Suki, we'd better get it over."

Julie gave her a look of vicious hate, quickly concealed by a mask of sugary sweetness.

"I don't know how you manage to be so charming!" she said quite mildly. "If I were you I shouldn't make one of those remarks to Mother. She doesn't understand modern young people like you. She'd think you were being rude."

Camilla went a fiery red and I pulled her after me, out of the room, before she could think of any other reply that would put her badly in the wrong. I had the feeling that that was exactly what Julie would have liked her to have done and that she was doing all in her power to engineer a situation that would make Gideon side with her against his sister.

"She'd *know* if I were being rude!" Camilla muttered crossly.

I could have shaken her. I slammed shut the door

into Gideon's room and stalked down the corridor to
where I imagined the reception rooms to be.

"For heaven's sake, Camilla!" I scolded her. "Can't
you see how she loves to put you in the wrong? You're
not helping Gideon, you know."

She gave me a sulky smile.

"I'm sorry," she said. "Come on, it's this way. Let's
beard the old dragon in her lair quickly, before Julie
persuades Gideon to stay."

"I don't think she'll manage to do that," I replied
with quiet confidence. And I really believed it. However
fond Gideon was of Julie, he would be worried about
his work and he would be back at the station as soon as
he possibly could be. It wasn't quite the reason I would
have liked, but I believed in facing facts. Gideon
would do many things for Camilla, but I was no more
than an employee and, as such, I scarcely impinged
on his consciousness.

Mrs. Burnett was half sitting, half lying on the sofa,
with a hand woven rug cast loosely over her knees. She
was very like Julie to look at, with the same soft hair,
grey instead of mauve, and the same soft skin and
innocent expression. But the years had written in lines
of discontent and disappointment beside the eyes and
in the wrinkles of the mouth.

"Come over here, my dears. Camilla, you can sit on
the stool and Miss King in the chair."

We obediently settled ourselves where she had suggested, while she looked from one to the other of us
with bland amusement.

"And what do you think of our remnant of the
British Raj?" she asked slyly.

Camilla managed to show her distaste by being far
too enthusiastic in a breathless voice.

"It's *lovely*! Were you really here before Independence?"

Mrs. Burnett winced. Independence didn't seem so
very long ago to her and she didn't like the fleeting

years being pushed on her so ruthlessly. She sighed in a way that was very reminiscent of her daughter.

"Oh yes, indeed. The wasted years, I often call them. I longed to go home to England, if only because of Julie. It was only right that she should have friends among her own kind and meet the right young men, but my husband is in love with India and *nothing* would make him leave. I think he would have died in England—can you understand that? He had lived for so long here that he would be quite out of place in an English provincial town, and London would have completely stifled him. Besides which, living in the sun, you know, does queer things to a man— But we won't think about that, will we?" She hesitated, obviously unsure as to how to continue. "It's so difficult for me to ask you this," she said at last. "But I should be so grateful if you would encourage Gideon to stay here for a few days. It's not for *my* sake, but Julie so seldom sees anyone of her own age."

Camilla stared at her with unblinking eyes.

"I don't think either of us could persuade Gideon one way or the other," I said as gently as I could. "Why don't you talk to him?"

Mrs. Burnett looked more upset than ever.

"I don't want him to think that we are trying to trap him into anything! Oh dear, how awkward everything is!"

I smiled sympathetically, trying to ignore the expression of outrage on Camilla's face.

"We're not so very far away and Julie comes over quite often," I put in comfortingly.

"It's not the same. She has no *opportunities* here, the poor dear."

Camilla could keep silent no longer.

"And so you deliberately trip up Gideon's horse!" she exclaimed.

Mrs. Burnett raised her delicately trimmed eyebrows.

"*I*? No, dear. How could I? I wasn't even playing. And anyway, it's a pony, not a horse."

Camilla cast her outraged glance on me.

"But *he* tripped Gideon up!"

"It doesn't matter, dear," I said hastily. "*Not now!*"

"But—" she began.

"But really there's nothing to say," I said firmly. "No one can make up Gideon's mind for him. Not even you!"

Mrs. Burnett looked sad and worried.

"I'm sure my husband meant it for the best," she said humbly. "He gets so worried about Julie too. You do understand, don't you?"

I felt rather sickened by the whole affair.

"It doesn't matter," I assured her in stifled tones. "Perhaps you will excuse us if we go back to Gideon now?"

Her eyes narrowed and she gave me a look of hatred that was so like her daughter that I gasped!

"I suppose you're after him yourself!" she snapped.

I eyed her helplessly, at a complete loss to know as to how to answer. But Camilla had none of my reservations.

"Suki wouldn't be so vulgar," she remarked with touching dignity. "Would you, Suki?"

I muttered something which could have been either yes or no, took one last despairing look round the too upholstered room, and fled down the passage to Gideon's bedroom. I rushed into his room without even bothering to knock. I felt stifled and dirtied by the scented air of the Burnetts and the kind of life they were trying to keep alive.

"Oh, Gideon!" I gulped.

He was very nice about it. He held both my hands reassuringly and the mocking look went out of his eyes, if not the smile.

"Well, well," he said. "How very flattering! I gather

your reactions to our hostess are exactly the same as Camilla's!"

I bit my lip. "It isn't that I don't like them," I hedged.

"No?"

"And it isn't Julie's fault, is it?" I went on with determined objectivity.

Gideon lost his smile and became serious for a while.

"That's the way I look at it," he said. "What chance has the girl ever had? Imagine being cooped up in this museum for long."

Considering that I agreed with him, I wondered why I should resent his interest in Julie so much. I pulled my hands free and sighed.

"Does that mean you're going to stay for a while?" I asked casually.

He gave me a lopsided grin.

"Not exactly. I have a job to do and I reckon I shall be able to do most of it on crutches—somehow. No, I thought perhaps we could have Julie over more often. She might like to come and stay for a spell. She could share the same house as you and Camilla."

"I suppose she could," I agreed gloomily.

"It wouldn't be for long, necessarily," he coaxed me.

I smiled deliberately and said with forced cheerfulness: "It won't matter to me anyhow! I shall be far too busy building my dam!"

"Oh?" he asked cautiously.

"It's all settled," I went on, the words tumbling over themselves. "I explained it all to the old men of the village and they were quite pleased!"

"Indeed?"

I remembered belatedly that his permission was still required and that I wasn't going the best way to get it.

"You do approve, don't you?" I asked him anxiously.

"I don't know," he replied dryly. "You'll have to tell me about it."

"Yes, I will," I assured him. "It won't cost very much at all. I really think you'll like the idea."

"Possibly," he said with complete lack of interest. "But in the meantime I want nothing so much as to go home."

With compassion I noticed the worn look on his face which had not been there earlier. We were all so interested in our own affairs that we had hardly had time to fully realise that he was the one who had been badly hurt.

"I'm sorry, Gideon."

His smile came back.

"I know you are. You're a soft-hearted creature." He began to struggle off the bed while I watched him worriedly.

"I think I'd better get some help," I suggested.

He nodded, concentrating hard on the sheer physical effort of gaining his balance.

"Get Camilla," he bade me. "And if you can, get the jeep round to the nearest door."

Camilla came running when I called her. She helped her brother across the room and towards the door that I had first come in by.

"I thought Julie was with you," she half-accused him. He leaned a little more heavily on her shoulder.

"To tell the truth I was in pain and wanted to be alone for a while," he told her. "She'll be along to say goodbye."

Mrs. Burnett came too, to wave goodbye to her parting guests. She put a possessive arm around her daughter's shoulders and hugged her close.

"It's been such fun having your friends for the day," she said brightly. "I do hope that poor boy is going to be all right, jolted over these rough roads. You must drive extra carefully, Miss King!"

It was quite a business getting Gideon installed in the jeep. Fortunately the front seat gave him plenty of room for his leg to stick out in front of him and there were a number of cushions that could be used as props. I looked at his ashen face with some anxiety, noticing afresh the lines of pain and his shadowed eyes that his determined smile was not really covering up.

"The sooner we go the better," I said to Camilla. She got into the back after shaking hands prettily with Mrs. Burnett. Julie she just ignored, and I was in two minds as to whether I ought to press her to at least say good-bye. But I need not have worried because Julie was not thinking of Camilla at all. Just as I was on the point of letting in the clutch, she made a rush at Gideon, flung her arms round his neck and kissed him warmly on the cheek.

"I'll be over first thing in the morning," she whispered to him. "It won't be so very long to wait, will it?"

I couldn't help noticing that he kissed her back.

"I'll be waiting for you, chicken," he said.

Julie flushed with pleasure and triumph and she graciously nodded her head to me.

"Be very careful of him, Susan. He means a great deal to me!" As if we hadn't all been made aware of that! I didn't say a word. I drove straight down the neglected drive and breathed a sigh of relief when we gained the public road.

"Did you hear that?" Camilla demanded in exasperated tones.

Gideon sat well back in his seat and closed his eyes.

"My, my," he said, "how you girls do carry on!" And I wondered if he meant Camilla and me or Julie Burnett. But somehow it seemed too much to hope that he meant the latter.

Gideon remained unbearable for the rest of the day. He lay in his bed and demanded that everybody went and paid him a visit at frequent intervals all through what was left of the evening. My turn came just as I was putting the finishing touches to my latest drawing of the dam I was going to build. I threw down my pencil, feeling thoroughly cross, and went across to the main house and his bedroom.

"I think you're having far too many visitors!" I greeted him.

He scowled at me through the gloom from the inadequate lamp.

"Is that possible? For heaven's sake, woman, stop staring at me and do something to make me a little more comfortable!"

I humped up his pillows and tried to straighten out the worst of the creases in his sheets.

"Why don't you give in and try to get some sleep?"

He snorted impatiently. "Does that mean you're ready for bed?" he demanded.

I smothered a yawn. "Not at all," I said very politely. "If you like, I'm quite prepared to entertain you for the greater part of the night."

He gave me a suspicious look and was only partly mollified by the innocent expression on my face.

"I suppose you'd better tell me about this dam of yours," he bribed me. I fell for the suggestion, hook, line and sinker. He grinned at me amiably. "Supposing you go and get the drawings," he suggested.

I eyed the black smudges under his eyes with some misgiving, but I went and got the drawings all the same. My enthusiasm for the project bubbled up inside me and I was doubly annoyed that I hadn't been able to finish the drawings off properly.

Gideon snatched the sheaf of papers from me and spread them out on his bed. I tried to explain the main points to him, but he brushed away my explanations preferring to see the thing as a whole for himself.

"Are you planning to line the reservoirs?" he asked.

I hesitated. "I'm not sure. Some of the soil around is clay."

"But it will lead to seepage?"

I nodded unhappily. "The trouble is the lining adds to the cost," I explained.

He glanced down at my figures. "I think it would prove less costly in the end than persistent seepage."

I nodded. It sounded as though he was getting keen as well and that was what I wanted at that moment, more than anything else in the world.

"What had you thought of using?" he asked me.

I pointed at yet another piece of paper.

"Possibly butyl. It's easy enough to lay. You just drag the sheets out flat and join them together."

"Or?"

"Or P.V.C. The sun might affect it, but if it's buried under about six inches of soil, with the edges covered even more carefully and compacted, I think it should last a goodish while. It has the advantage of being about a third of the cost of the other and the labour costs of laying it here shouldn't be so very great."

"No," he agreed. "We can pick up enough cheap labour to do the whole thing in a few days. The difficulty will be in getting the materials."

"I'll get them," I assured him doggedly. "I'll get them if it's the last thing I do!"

Gideon lay back, suddenly exhausted.

"It may very well be!" he said. "You'd better take a trip to Delhi and see what you can do!"

I sat very still, scarcely daring to breathe.

"Do you mean I can go ahead?"

He grinned. "I don't see why not," he said.

I couldn't sleep at all that night. Every time I turned out the light, I thought of yet another point to do with the dam. By the grey light of dawn I had modified the whole project into a much more sensible unit that had the potential to water most of the research station and not just the two fields on either side of the turgid stream. A wretched bird that I had never heard before came just outside my window and mocked my restlessness. It was not a songbird in the accepted sense, for its repertoire consisted of a series of strange and intermittent shrieks that sounded more like someone being murdered. I buried myself in my pillow and tried to ignore it, and within a few seconds I was fast asleep.

I awoke only because Camilla was pinching the lobe of my ear. Resentfully, I struggled to get free, but she was persistent, and slowly I pulled myself into full consciousness.

"What do you want?" I asked grumpily.

Camilla laughed. "Considering it's nearly lunch-time—"

"*Lunch-time*!" I sat up hastily and stared at her. "It can't be!"

"Oh, but it is! And brother Gideon would like to see you when you can spare him the time."

I gave an abashed glance at the plans of the dam that had fallen on the floor by my bed.

"Did he say that?" I asked, thinking that I recognised Gideon's touch in the words.

Camilla nodded vigorously. Her eyes were lit with laughter, and immediately I was suspicious.

"What's up?" I asked.

"What should be up? Apart from the fact that you're so late that it's hardly worth your while beginning a day's work!"

I ignored that, feeling rather ashamed of myself. When I put my feet on the floor and stood up, I felt heavy and immobile as one does when one has slept too deeply after a restless night.

"How is Gideon?" I asked quite grumpily. If it had not been for him I would have got to bed at a more reasonable time and I could have rounded up the *panchayat* by now and told them that I had his approval.

"Like a bear with a sore head, only it's his leg." Camilla lost the happy note in her voice for an instant. "I do hope that doctor set it properly!"

I was hoping so too. I dressed in a hurry, splashing cold water on to my face to make sure I was properly filled with sudden tears and for the moment I didn't want to go because Gideon wouldn't be in Delhi. I tried to put him out of my mind—to think of anything else, but the picture of him as I had last seen him, trying to hide the fact that he was in pain and concerned because he was sending a woman on her own into a foreign city, persisted despite my best efforts. I turned my face away from Camilla because I could feel myself blushing and I knew it was not beyond her to find the reason why.

"It's terribly hot!" I murmured.

Camilla gave me a sympathetic grin. "Terribly!"

A pedlar, selling copper and brass and a few silver bracelets, came hurrying over to us.

"The *memsahibs* would like to buy?" he whined.

Camilla brushed him away impatiently, but I was curious to see his goods. The silver of the bangles was not very pure, but they were pretty and intricately designed. I asked him how much they were, but I never heard the answer. The engine suddenly whistled with all its might and Joseph came running down the platform and practically threw me into the train.

"It's leaving!" he shouted. "Good luck!"

I waved to them both, the tears stinging my eyes again. A multitude of hangers-on grasped the outside of the train so that I could hardly see the vanishing platforms with their inadequate shelter. In a moment I could see nothing at all and settled a little unhappily into my seat, trying not to think about Gideon at all, or anything to do with him.

"Forgive me for interrupting you," my next-door neighbour said after a while. "There is someone in the corridor who is trying to attract your attention."

I looked first at my neighbour, a gentleman in a dirty dun-coloured turban. His smile was charmingly decorated with a variety of gold-filled teeth and his fingers were bedecked with a number of large-stoned rings. He smiled and nodded out to the corridor. Stand-

ing there, looking in at me and grinning all over his
face, stood Joseph.

I stood up hastily and struggled with the door into
the corridor.

"What are you doing here?" I demanded when it at
last gave way to the insistent pressure of my hand.
"What have you done with Camilla?"

His grin grew broader.

"She stayed behind to look after Gideon, but we
agreed that somebody had to go with you, so I was
elected."

"Does Gideon know?" I asked with grim foreboding.

"Good heavens, no! He'll probably sack me when
I get back!"

Or me, I reflected bitterly. It would be far more
likely to be me. He would never believe that I had
never been a party to this mad, stupid idea! Never,
never! For I had to admit that I could hardly believe
it myself, that they would play such a stupid trick
without my consent. And I didn't want Joe with me.
There was nothing for him to do in Delhi and I was
more than capable of looking after myself.

"I don't know where you're going to sit," I said
coldly. "All the seats in my compartment are taken."

He looked at me, astonishment slowly taking the
place of his pleasure.

"Aren't you *pleased*?" he demanded.

"No, I am not!" I snapped. "Gideon is going to be
furious. What did you think you could gain by such
idiotic behaviour?"

He shrugged uncomfortably.

"It didn't seem right to let you go on your own—
and besides," he went on dolefully, "I thought you'd
want me to be with you."

And in a way I did, I supposed. I mean that I was
glad to know that I should have someone to share the
responsibility of finding my way about Old Delhi, even
if I did feel that I could manage New Delhi quite well

on my own. I suppose, too, I was glad to have Joseph's company. He was my friend and we had sealed the fact with a kiss, and in a way he reminded me of Timothy, and anything that could do that was welcome at the moment. No, the only problem was Gideon's fury. That he would be extremely angry, I never had the slightest doubt. Our only hope was that he would have expended most of his fury on Camilla before we ever got back. But that was a forlorn hope, because his very real sense of justice would soon know that it had had very little to do with her—that Joseph and I were old enough to make our own decisions as to how we managed things. And the truth was that this wasn't very well managed at all! There would be gossip and I wouldn't be able to prevent it. And Joseph would be away from his work for no reason at all, and that was unforgivable.

"Oh yes," I said tartly, "I shall *love* having you with me when I think of Gideon struggling to manage on his own with a broken leg! I shall love it still more when he sacks the two of us—and we shall have deserved it!" I went back to my seat and sat down in it, uncomfortably aware that I hadn't been particularly kind when all Joseph had been trying to do was to make things easier for me.

He followed me into the compartment, frowning at my companions as if he were hoping to frighten them out of their seats.

"Surely you aren't afraid of Gideon?" he asked me resentfully when nobody stirred.

I glared at him, trying to remind him with my eyes that we were not the only people who could speak English.

"I respect him," I said tightly. "Joseph, do go and find yourself a seat!"

He went, but I was no happier left alone. My neighbour tried to engage me in conversation, but somehow I didn't have much to say. I was obsessed by my own emotions, by my own misery. Nothing that Gideon could ever say to me was worse than my own imaginings during the first half of that journey. How could Joseph have been so stupid?

I was still downright sulky when Joseph came to tell me that we could have lunch on the train.

"I thought there wasn't a restaurant car?" I said, surprised.

"There isn't exactly," he admitted. "I got off and bought some things from one of the station vendors at the last stop."

I must say I was very glad that I hadn't known about it. To have Joseph on the train at all was bad enough, but to lose him somewhere in India would have been too much altogether.

"There's more room where I am," Joseph persuaded me. "I'll carry your things and then we can be together."

It seemed churlish to refuse, so I spent the rest of the journey sitting beside him and chatting of this and that. On the whole it was very much better than being on my own, and as his compartment was air-conditioned while mine had not been, my temper began to improve and I started to enjoy myself. When we came into Delhi I was astonished by how quickly the journey had gone and the feeling of nervous excitement that had been with me ever since Gideon had said I could go ahead with the dam came back again with a rush.

"Supposing I've got my figures all wrong!" I wailed to Joseph.

He grinned. "Well, supposing you have?"

I grabbed my suitcase and followed him down on to the platform.

"You'll have to check them for me before we do any ordering," I said.

His grin became positively triumphant. "Okay, I will," he said.

He grabbed my suitcase with his free hand and

started off down the platform with his ticket firmly
lodged in his teeth. He had to stand and wait for me on
the other side of the barrier while I searched for mine
in my handbag. When I had finally given it up to the
collector, he had already found a taxi and was telling
the driver the name of the hotel we wanted to go to.

＊　　　＊　　　＊

> *"If there be a paradise on earth,*
> *'Tis here! 'Tis here! 'Tis here!"*

Joseph found the famous Persian quotation on the
walls of the Hall of Private Audience in the Red Fort,
the room which had once held the famous Peacock
Throne, in its more glamorous days, when the ceiling
too had been of solid silver. He quoted the words softly,
with a touch of magic, as though he had only just discovered their meaning and that it was somehow wrapped up with the fact that I was with him. I gazed up
at the flowing script that spelt out the original words
and tried to remember that it was only because time
was at a standstill that I was so confused about what I
felt and thought, that in fact I was waiting for
Timothy.

Joseph took me by the hand and led me towards the
Florentine panels, the only one of which I can remember
depicted Orpheus playing for the birds.

"You are enjoying this, aren't you?" he asked me.
"You would never have come here on your own, would
you?"

"No," I agreed, "probably not."

"Then you would have missed one of the finest sights
in the world!" he concluded enthusiastically. "If we
had it back home in the States, so many people would
be falling over themselves to see it it would pay off the
National Debt all by itself!"

I grinned, amused by the idea. It had obviously not
occurred to him that if you took such a gorgeous palace

out of its own setting you would reduce its conception to a tourist's nine-day wonder just like any other. It was the history that spoke through the magnificent walls and the miracle of carvings on the walls, a history that had lived and suffered and had formed part of the race memory of the people. You couldn't ship history around the world with the marble and the stone.

We walked past the marble stall of the emperor's Grand Vizier which stood in front of the throne dais and went on into the private apartments and through into the Rang Mahal, or Painted Palace.

Joseph gave me a mocking smile.

"This is a very appropriate setting for you," he said.

I was intrigued by the central marble basin through which runs a water channel passing right through the palace, its bottom carved in the shape of a lotus flower. It was known as the Canal of Paradise.

"Do I look so much in need of a bath?" I retorted lightly.

Joseph stood back to allow me to pass ahead of him into the royal bathrooms, the *hammams*, exquisite Mogul and therefore Moslem baths, similar in function to our Turkish baths, but for them an essential part of the preparation for solemn prayer. It was no surprise therefore that a short way away stood the Pearl Mosque, designed by Aurangzeb, one of the Mogul rulers, for his personal use and for that of the royal ladies at his court. It was too ornate for my taste and I was glad when we escaped its sugary atmosphere into the gardens outside.

"There is something to be said for purdah," Joseph went on. "I should like to keep you away from the anxieties of working and having to provide for yourself and keep you myself alone."

I was shocked by the very idea.

"Oh, would you?" I said haughtily. "Well, let me tell you the price would be very much too high!"

He grinned and put his arm round my waist. It was very uncomfortable walking along like that, but I hadn't got the heart to set myself free from the casual embrace.

"I wonder?" he speculated. "Wouldn't you really rather like to be petted and privileged?"

I gave the question serious thought, but my independence was too valuable to me for me to be able to turn my back on it, even verbally. It seemed I was fully committed to standing on my own feet.

"No, I'd hate it," I replied simply.

The pressure on my wrist became stronger and he turned me in the circle of his arms to face him.

"I think I could change your mind," he said abruptly. He pulled me closer and tried to kiss me on the mouth. At another time I might have suffered the kiss with better fortitude, but at that moment I was only conscious of the fact that I was hot and that I didn't want to be touched.

"Please don't, Joe," I said gently.

"What? Change your mind?"

I shook my head.

"Please don't kiss me. I don't feel like it."

His pride was hurt and I was sorry. To cover the awkward moment I bent over and picked a flower that was struggling for life despite the heat and I put it in his buttonhole with a flourish. We exchanged slightly embarrassed laughs, both aware that we were not the right people in the right moment, despite the beauty all around us. Almost as if he had come to order one of the Sikh guides, in his white jodphurs and tweed jacket, came across to us over the burnt grass.

"Do you wish a guide?" he asked.

Joseph shook his head. "We have already seen all that we want to."

The guide was unconvinced.

"That is impossible, *sahib*. You have not been here

at night when the moon hangs over the palace and little lamps are placed in the niches of the two pavilions. The whole romance of India breathes in this garden then!"

Joseph gave me a sardonic look. I wondered if he had it in mind to bring me back that evening, but I need not have concerned myself. Joseph had only one intention and that was to get rid of the guide as quickly as possible. He was always embarrassed by people asking for *baksheesh*, even when it was justified, and this worry was apt to take precedence over all others.

"Let's go," he whispered to me.

It seemed a pity to depart so soon, but I gave way as gracefully as I could. Timothy had long ago taught me not to argue on these occasions—though in those days I have to admit that it would never have even occurred to me to argue with him. I had learned quite a lot since coming to India.

"Perhaps those other people would like a guide," I suggested as another small group of Europeans came out into the gardens. The guide looked over his shoulder to where I was pointing, saluted smartly, and went off to ask them. Joe took a look at them and went quite white in the face.

"What's she doing here?" he demanded between clenched teeth.

I took a closer look at the little group and was surprised to recognise Julie's blue-pink hair.

"Perhaps it's her twin," I whispered.

"No such luck!" Joseph exclaimed.

And at that moment she saw us too.

"Why, look who's here!" she exclaimed in her 'little girl' voice. "They're friends of Gideon's! Well, not friends exactly, but they work with him!"

Her companions glanced at us without too much warmth.

"That fellow who runs the research station?" one of them asked.

Julie's lips tightened angrily. "He's very important in our locality!" she said sternly.

They grinned at her, humouring her. It was obvious that they didn't think anything was important but their own interests.

"Of course! Quite agree!" they murmured.

I was the one who wanted to go then. I forced myself to look dispassionately at Julie and I had to admit she was very pretty. She was busy proving how loyal she was to Gideon. So the only reason why I couldn't find it within me to like her was because I was jealous of her, and that I didn't really like to admit.

"What are you doing in Delhi?" I asked her.

She turned to me immediately and smiled quite charmingly.

"I was so worried about Gideon that my parents thought it would be better for me to get away for a while. I'm staying here with friends." She smiled again, quickly and impersonally. "And you?"

I explained about the dam we were building, trying hard not to get carried away by my own enthusiasm. Julie was not very interested. Her eyes kept sliding over to Joseph as if she wanted to know what he was doing with me, but didn't quite like to ask.

"It must be nice to be able to take a look round while you're here," she said instead.

"It is," I agreed. "We didn't have much time to see Delhi when we passed through when we first came."

Julie sniffed.

"I can't imagine enjoying it much here myself if it weren't for the social life," she said. "It used to be much better, of course, when the British were here in force, but it's still very much better than anywhere else."

I laughed.

"We haven't much time for parties," I admitted. "We had a quite exhausting morning trying to arrange for all the stuff we want to be sent to the research station quickly—"

"Gideon should have come," she cut me off. "Gideon knows everyone here, so there wouldn't have been any trouble." She lowered her voice and whispered in my ear, "What on earth induced you to bring that American? *He* wouldn't be much use!"

There was an awkward silence. Joe had not been particularly helpful that morning. He had obligingly checked my figures, but that had led to his having ideas of his own as to how the dam should be built and we had very nearly quarrelled over the arrangements I had already made. He hadn't been much help in finding the various dealers either, but I had been glad of his presence just the same. It had been nice to know he was there in case anything went wrong. And there had been a lot of things to go wrong and most of them had through various misunderstandings and my complete lack of knowledge about the various government controls.

"Don't you like him?" I asked sweetly, taking the war firmly into the enemy's camp. Julie, however, was not to be so easily put out.

"Oh, I'm quite indifferent, my dear. He's not exactly *important* in any way, is he?"

"Perhaps not," I said.

She looked at me even more closely, screwing up her eyes as if she were a trifle short-sighted.

"I don't really understand you at all!" she complained breathlessly. "I suppose it's because all professional women are so terribly efficient and *unfeeling*! I mean we have so much more time to care about people, haven't we? You have your job to consider first all the time, and having to compete with men in their own sphere. I'm so glad that I don't have to bother with all that!"

I found that I resented the idea that I was unfeminine more than I liked.

"Most women have jobs of some sort nowadays," I said pacifically.

Her eyes glinted. "I'm afraid my father would never allow me to *work*," she said with a tinkling laugh. "Don't your people miss you when you are so far away from them?"

I shrugged my shoulders, refusing to answer.

"Dear, dear," she said. "Poor Gideon! When I get back I shall see that he has some *fun*! I can tell that he doesn't get much with you and Joseph around. I don't suppose you ever talk about anything else but your work and plant diseases. How dull he must be!"

I bit my lip, almost sure that she was right. Poor Gideon probably could do with some light relief, but I didn't think the Burnetts were the right ones to achieve this. It had already cost Gideon one broken leg.

One of the men who had come with Julie pulled at her arm to attract her attention.

"Are we going to stand around here all day?" he asked her plaintively. "Surely you see enough of these two when you're at home!"

Julie tossed her head so that her pale mauve hair was lifted in the wind. It was a very pretty and very well-rehearsed gesture.

"Hush, sweet! One has to be polite!" She giggled, maliciously aware that her remark had been hurtful.

The young man pulled her away, kissing her on the cheek as he did so. She bridled and giggled again, pleasantly embarrassed by his attention. I hope I didn't look as disapproving as I felt.

"Goodbye, Miss Burnett," I said formally. "We shall be going home tonight so I don't expect we shall run into each other again in Delhi."

She frowned at me. I think she was wondering if I would carry tales back to Gideon, but apparently she came to the conclusion that even if I did he wouldn't believe me.

"I don't suppose we shall see much of each other— ever," she said simply. "But if we do just you remember that my motto is *tit for tat*!"

So that was it! I grinned wryly to myself. There wasn't much I could find to admire in Miss Julie Burnett.

"Ouch!" Joseph broke into my disagreeable thoughts. "That girl gives me the creeps. What does Gideon see in her?"

I pursed my lips together and said nothing at all. I was battling with the knowledge that I could have cheerfully kicked Julie. And I preferred not to even *think* about what Gideon could see in her. When she tossed her head in that particular way and smiled up at any man as if she regarded him as some Olympic hero, I should have thought it was only too obvious!

"Oh well," said Joseph. "It doesn't matter to us, thank God! We aren't important enough to be troubled by her."

I wished I could comfort myself so easily.

On the train that night I simply could not get to sleep. The air-conditioned compartment had been speedily and easily converted into a sleeping cabin. It was comfortable and cool. The attendant had wrought this transformation while Joe and I had been dining in the dining-car that was attached to the train and which served both Indian and English dishes. He had been waiting in the corridor when I had come back to check if there was anything else I wanted.

"The *sahib* is in another car as he requested," he told me. "Is there anything further I can get you before I attend to him?"

I shook my head and tipped him as he was obviously hoping that I would.

"Goodnight, *memsahib*," he had bowed and had sketched a vague salute, carrying his hand to his turban as he left, and I had been alone.

To entertain myself I had chased a couple of beetles back into the corridor from which they had dared to enter my compartment and I had played with the mos-

I shook my head.

"It wasn't that," I explained. "In fact he suggested that I should come. But since I've been here, I've hardly had time to write to *him,* and I suppose that makes a difference."

He gave me a long, hard look.

"I suppose it could," he agreed. I noted the careful change in wording and blushed. I didn't want him to think that I had made all the running as far as Timothy was concerned.

"He—he won't have much to say about his work, you see," I rushed into speech. "He knows that I don't understand much about what he's doing."

Gideon looked thoughtful.

"And he doesn't understand anything about you at all?" he suggested mildly.

"Oh, I wouldn't say that! He was always very kind!" I insisted. "I should never have passed my exams if he hadn't coached me and taken an interest."

"Which hardly makes you the love of his life," Gideon went on firmly. "Why don't you write to him and break off that disastrous arrangement you made between you?"

I tried once again to remember exactly what it was I had felt for Timothy, but memory will play the oddest tricks. I could remember exactly the brand of stomach powder that worked most effectively and I could remember his favourite tunes, most of them classical and rather on the serious side. It came as rather a shock to know that it wouldn't hurt at all if I never saw Timothy again. But I couldn't say so. I certainly couldn't admit anything of the sort to Gideon. Why, in a way it was my only defence, my only weapon against the pale blue attraction of Julie Burnett. I had to keep things firmly in proportion, and that meant remembering that she was the one who was attractive to Gideon—not me. And it was important to remember this all the time.

"It was a very vague arrangement," I said with a laugh. "But I guess I must be the faithful type!"

Gideon snorted. "How you love your illusions!"

I was hurt and I showed it.

"Don't you think I can be loyal?" I demanded.

"I wasn't questioning *that*," he scoffed. "What I wonder is if you really know your own mind. And that I seriously doubt!"

I was furiously angry.

"I am over twenty-one!" I informed him haughtily.

But he only laughed. "Go on, get out and go and make your arrangements. I want to get my bearer to make me a little more comfortable!"

"Couldn't I help you before I go?" I asked, immediately solicitous.

"No, you cannot!" he retorted. "You'd like messing about far too much for my comfort!"

"Oh, indeed?" I said coldly. "Then be uncomfortable. I don't care! I don't have to sleep in that bird's nest!"

His eyes lit with amusement.

"And aren't you glad?" he teased me.

But it wasn't the sort of teasing that I was in the mood for, so I beat a hasty retreat before either of us said something that neither of us would be able to forget.

Later, I happened to be passing Gideon's door when he was seeing Joseph and finding out from him why he had gone to Delhi with me. It was a very different kind of interview and I couldn't help wondering why I had been let off so lightly. But then perhaps he knew that it had been Joseph's idea and that I hadn't known a thing about it until after the train had pulled out of the station.

It was a moment of great pride when I stood on the edge of the wheat field and dug the first spadeful of earth into the wheelbarrow. The dam project had begun.

A variety of Indian labour had come from far and wide to dig the reservoirs, some of them, to my great satisfaction, had actually been sent by their own villages to see how it was done. Joseph suggested that I made a speech, but I was too stuffed up with emotion to say anything at all. Instead, I sat on the bank of the sluggish stream and allowed myself to dream of its future glory. The first of the monsoon rains were not very far away and then we should see the waters swell and slowly gather into the two tanks, offering undreamed-of crops in the future. I hugged the knowledge to me with glee. Whatever I was going to suffer personally when the time came for me to leave India, at least I would have left something behind me that was worthwhile and lasting.

The *panchayat* stood in solemn assembly on the opposite bank worrying about the costs and their own disbelief that a slip of a girl could organise anything on the kind of scale they were expecting. From my side of the stream I could afford to smile and wave to them. To my surprise, and with tremendous dignity, they responded with a bow and waved back.

"Look at them! As proud as peacocks!" Joseph scoffed.

"They have something to be proud about!" I retorted crossly. I was getting rather fond of this group of stiff-necked old men despite myself.

"It wasn't their idea!"

"No," I agreed, "but they allowed it to happen. That's quite something in itself!"

Joe shook his head. "They've got you thinking in terms of symbolic action too!"

"Maybe," I laughed. "But this symbol has to be one of better things to be. And it will be too! You just wait and see."

Joseph shrugged, visibly depressed.

"If I'm here for long enough," he grunted. "The

great white chief is after my hide after my going to Delhi with you."

I was sympathetic, but I couldn't pretend to be exactly surprised.

"Well, you did ask for it rather, didn't you?"

The hint of weakness in his face was exaggerated by the anger that burned up within him.

"He should never have sent you on your own in the first place! It was an iniquitous thing to do!"

I leaped to Gideon's defence, feeling decidedly ruffled.

"How can you say so?" I gave him a rather sharp, remembering glance. "Who did all the arranging, anyway?"

It wasn't particularly kind, I suppose, and he flushed angrily.

"It still wasn't right that you should go on your own," he persisted. "I told him so too!"

"And what did he say?" I asked curiously. I had heard enough of the two men's conversation to know that it was angry, but I hadn't been able to hear what they had actually said.

Joseph shrugged his shoulders.

"I guess I'd better not tell you," he rumbled. "Not that I agree with a word he said, but I don't suppose he meant me to repeat it all to you."

"Perhaps not," I said stiffly, "as it was obviously something unpleasant!"

He flushed. "I didn't say that!" he denied indignantly. "As a matter of fact it wasn't anything against you at all. It was me he was angry with!"

I said no more, but I was now well aware of the danger signals being up between the two men. And I had no doubt as to who had the right of the matter. That was Gideon, for he was a fair man and not given to being carried away by his emotions as Joseph was only too often.

It was something of a relief when one or two of the

old men summoned me to join them on their side of the stream. Joseph showed no signs of coming with me, and I was glad, though I was slightly ashamed of being so, because he had had difficulty in getting on with them recently. He considered them reactionary and they considered him brash. There was something to be said for both opinions.

"Are you sure it will be ready before the rains?" the old men asked me anxiously.

I assumed a confidence I was far from feeling.

"Oh yes!" I said. "It will be a terrific amount of work because the ground is so hard, but everybody is very willing. We shall do it all right."

The leader of the *panchayat,* a very old man with flowing white hair, smiled into his beard.

"Who would have believed that a woman could speak with such confidence?" he scoffed gently. "Nevertheless, the *Sahib* says you are to be trusted and will make great things come to pass in our village. This evening we shall honour the gods and gain their favour as the women have been doing all day."

I thanked him warmly, secretly thrilled to bits that Gideon should have shown such trust in me. I left him, glowing with pleasure, just in time to see Gideon himself arriving in the passenger seat of his jeep which was driven by the *Swami.*

I ran towards them, waving to them as I went. Their unexpected presence was very reassuring and it was as much as I could do to refrain from throwing my arms round Gideon's neck.

"How lovely!" I exclaimed as I drew up to them. "I didn't think there was any way for you to come."

Gideon smiled at the *Swami.* "He brought me," he said. "He knew I wouldn't want to miss the great event! How's it going?"

"The ground is a bit hard," I said.

Gideon grunted. "We'll soon see about that!" he promised. Somehow he managed to get down to where the men were working and in a few seconds he had them organised into gangs and they were really putting their backs into moving the earth. The *Swami* and I stood and watched him.

"I do hope he doesn't hurt himself," I remarked, unable to keep my anxiety to myself any longer. "He's a grand man, isn't he?"

The *Swami* smiled his consent.

"He is my friend," he said.

Something in his smile made me wonder if I had been too effusive and had somehow given myself away —though what was there to give away beyond the fact that I liked and admired Gideon and was glad to be working for him? I refused to even think about anything else. Women, if they were wise, did not until they received some encouragement from a man. And I was wise enough to know the ways that led to heartbreak and despair, even if I wasn't wise enough to know that those ways can't always be avoided.

"Where is the other English young lady?" the *Swami* asked me, uncannily mirroring my own thoughts.

"Julie? She's in Delhi," I answered briefly.

The *Swami* swept his orange robe more closely round his shoulders.

"She is not the one for Gideon," he said decisively. "It would be a pity if he fell into the trap of thinking that she were. One needs compassion, but not for one's wife."

Of course, I reminded myself, the *Swami* was a wise man and accustomed to making prophetic utterances and interfering in other people's affairs, but I was still shy of him and not at all inclined to ask his advice.

"Her family sent her to Delhi so that she could get over Gideon's broken leg," I remarked sourly.

"A bribe. I expect she was shocked," he remarked cryptically.

"What do you mean?" I asked him, intrigued.

"It is more what I imagine," he replied. "I think I

had better assist Gideon back to the car." He turned to face me and I was terribly conscious of his fine head topped by his shock of wild, unkempt hair. "It is a good task you have set yourself here. India has great need of such ideas and such people." Then he was gone, running down the slope to where the men were working, exchanging a word with this one and patting another one on his shoulder. When he came to Gideon he said nothing at all, but offered him his shoulder as an extra crutch and almost tenderly helped him back into the jeep and drove away, back to the village and his bed.

That evening the whole village was astir. Little lights, kept going with little more than a dab of oil, lit up the hot, dusty streets, transforming them into a fairy paradise. Now and again a firework lit up the sky, whizzing and banging its way to extinction. The noisier, the better they were liked, and the Catherine Wheels that rose and zipped, revolving like a world gone mad, were the confirmed favourites of everybody. The village had decided to hold a feast, to appease the local household gods, and to have a lovely excuse for dousing each other with water and coloured dyes, a ceremony usually reserved for rather later in the year.

I wandered down the main shopping street looking at the sights. By the village well was the local goddess, patronised mostly by expectant mothers, which smelt usually of rancid ghee, a kind of purified butter that the women offered as a libation to ease their labour pains. Now it was covered by coloured streamers and garlands of marigolds lay at her feet while more of them formed an orange carpet before her. It was a very pretty sight.

Seeing me on my own, Lakshmi came across to me and stood by my side.

"Are you enjoying the festival?" she asked me. "Why isn't the *Sahib* with you?"

I laughed.

"The *Sahib* is having trouble carrying his leg around with him!" I told her. "But aren't the lights pretty? And why are the flowers all marigolds?"

She shrugged her shoulders.

"They are always marigolds. When we greet visitors we place garlands of marigolds round their necks; when we visit Ghandiji's memorial place we drop marigolds on the ground. In a way they are the national flower of India."

I accepted her explanation because in a way they suited India. The colour was brash and effective and refused point blank to be ignored, and the marigold was a common flower, easily grown and without the distinction of a sophisticated perfume to please the more jaded palate. A quieter bloom would droop in the hot sun or would be unable to withstand the long days of pelting rain in the monsoon, and it would therefore never summon up the spice and the will for survival that was all I knew of Mother India.

"I see," I said. "No one gave me a garland of marigolds when I arrived!"

Lakshmi giggled.

"When the dam is finished they'll give you hundreds!" she promised rashly. "The crops will grow and we'll be the richest village for miles around. We are all very pleased and proud. I am especially proud, of course!"

"Oh, why?" I asked.

She gave me a sidelong glance that was at once shy and teasing.

"Because it is I who serve you, why else?" she commented. Another rocket streaked through the black sky and fell practically at our feet, causing us both to laugh. "That is nothing yet!" she assured me. "You wait until later when we really get going!"

"Lakshmi—" I began, and then I stopped. After all, the question I wanted to ask her was personal and she might very well resent it.

"You want to ask something?" she prompted me.

"Well, yes," I said. "Why don't you go to one of the cities? You speak English so well. I'm sure you would make more money!"

She laughed softly.

"I have little need of money," she said. "Compared to my friends I am rich, and soon, when I marry, my home will be near here. Why should I go away?"

My interest was immediately caught.

"But who are you going to marry?" I asked, intrigued.

She laughed again, shrugging her shoulders a little.

"I do not know yet. My family are still considering the matter. All I know is that it is time for me to marry and that the money I earn will make me a fine dowry."

I felt sharply that she would never fall in love and never know the agony of indecision that I was going through. It seemed unfair somehow, for the glory of the occasional moment far outweighed the morose sorrow of knowing that Gideon would never fall in love with me.

"But don't you ever want to choose your own husband?" I asked her.

"Sometimes," she agreed lightly, "and sometimes not. The old ways are better when you have a good family and they are kind to you. I will have many years in which to fall in love with my husband."

Another sparkler roared through the sky and fell over Lakshmi's sister's house. It made me think of the poverty of that family and I could hardly bear the thought of Lakshmi being destined for the same sort of existence. As if she had read my thoughts, she smiled at me.

"Don't worry, I am what you would call in your country a 'good catch.' My family have worked very hard so that I shall marry well!"

"Marry well, yes!" I couldn't help arguing. "But what about marrying happily?"

Lakshmi was confused by the very idea and hung her head, only cheering up when I suggested that we should go back to the main bungalow for dinner before the festival really got under way. She walked back along the street with me and accompanied me on to the verandah.

"I shall go and tell the *Sahib* you are here," she said softly, and disappeared inside, leaving me alone with my thoughts. And they were not very comfortable ones, because I had grown fond of Lakshmi and I couldn't see that there was going to be much happiness in the future for either of us.

I chose the most comfortable chair on the verandah and sat down in it, luxuriously stretching my tired body. It had been quite a day and the softness of the night was very conducive to dreaming. In the distance I could smell something cooking, but I was not hungry enough for it to disturb me. Not even the thought of failing to get the dam finished before the rains came could really worry me and I was nearly asleep when Joseph came and joined me.

"Where's Camilla?" he asked.

I shook my head. "I don't know. She's probably with Gideon."

Joseph went and stood on the edge of the verandah, jingling his keys and a coin or two together in his pocket. After a while he began to whistle some endless tune under his breath.

"Do you have to?" I complained.

He ended with a note that even he could hear was off-key.

"Sorry." He scuffed his shoes on the top of the steps and jingled his keys some more. "Suki," he said at last, "I'm not getting anywhere, am I?"

I sat up with a jerk.

"What *do* you mean?"

He smiled wryly, coming close to the lamp, so that I had a completely new view of his face, lit up from below and giving him new and fascinating shadows. Unfortunately it only served to show that basic weakness about the mouth that I had always been aware of.

"You know quite well. I'm not exactly making a success of my time here, as the *Sahib* Gideon was kind enough to point out to me. You're getting all the kudos for your go-ahead vision with the dam and, damn it all, irrigation is supposed to be my field!"

"Well, so it is," I said in matter-of-fact tones. "What have you been doing about it?"

He was moodily silent for a long moment.

"You know perfectly well that I haven't done a thing about it," he said at last. "I've had my hands full with our wretched machinery."

"That's your job too," I reminded him. "You're also the mechanic."

He laughed harshly. "And I suppose you agree with him that I haven't been doing that very well either?"

"I didn't say that."

"You didn't have to," he said gloomily. "I can feel it in the air about me."

"Aren't you exaggerating just a little?" I teased him.

"You might think so, I don't! The only person who has any time for me at all at the moment is Camilla."

I was determinedly cheerful. "Hence your anxiety to know where she is?"

He nodded. "I thought she might like to watch the fireworks with me. I think she's the only person I could bear to have with me, quite honestly. At least she isn't perpetually nagging me to be something that I'm not!"

I sighed. I was puzzled that he should be even more gloomy now than he had been earlier.

"Have you had another session with Gideon?" I asked.

"Wouldn't you like to know!" he retorted bitterly. "You're not even grateful that I stuck out my neck for you by going to Delhi. Women!" he added almost as if it were a swear-word.

I stood up. He had successfully destroyed my moment of dreamy comfort in the chair. Now I only felt that I was at a disadvantage by being so much lower than he was. When I was standing up at least I could meet him on level terms.

"I was grateful," I said clearly. "But I'm not going to fall over myself to prove it to you."

His eyes sparkled with contempt in the light of the lamp.

"No, no. Never be seen fraternising with those who are out of favour! Funny, I had you figured out quite differently. I had a picture of you as a sweet English girl, loyal and without too much ambition. But you're not like that, are you? You're crowing your head off that Gideon's bought your scheme for the dam. But don't crow too hard. If the monsoon is early, your cheap little success will come crashing round your ears and your stature will be no higher in the great man's eyes than mine is now!"

I bit my lip, feeling slightly sick. I had been quite unprepared for anything like this from Joseph.

"You're jealous!" I accused him sharply, the tactless remark rising almost unbidden to my lips.

"Of course I'm jealous!" he agreed. "But I wouldn't have cared as much if you'd been different about it. I thought you were my friend!"

"I thought so too," I said coolly. "You're making it rather impossible, though, aren't you?"

"Am I?" He eyed me sardonically. "I'm not the one who's been spilling tales to Gideon!"

"Meaning that I have?" I demanded.

"Haven't you?"

"Not that I'm aware of!" I denied sharply. "Look, Joe, what is all this?"

He hunched up his shoulders and sat heavily in the nearest chair.

"The jeep wouldn't start again. The *Swami* had to get it going with his own fair hands. It seems he was a mechanic himself before he took to being a holy man instead. Never cease to surprise one, do they? I mean, who would have thought that he ever earned his living just like everyone else? Well, anyway, it was just about the final straw as far as Gideon was concerned. I rather gathered that not even you could find much use for me."

I was uneasily aware of a feeling of acute irritation that he couldn't keep the vehicles properly maintained and I wondered just what it was that Gideon had said to him.

"I haven't said anything," I said.

"Well, I did," he said moodily. "I even told him about our running into Julie in Delhi. *That* set him back a bit, I might tell you."

"The *Swami* doesn't think she's the right person for Gideon either," I said without thought.

He flung back his head and laughed.

"I suppose you're planning to cut her out!" he exclaimed. "You might just manage it if you play your cards right!"

I gave him a look of extreme distaste.

"Gideon doesn't see me like that!" I passed it off casually. But for some reason my heart was suddenly pounding within me. "It wouldn't be fitting anyway," I said gruffly.

For answer Joseph laughed again.

"Well, well," he said, "whoever would have thought it?"

CHAPTER TEN

IF I was pleased when Camilla came and joined us, Joseph most certainly was not.

"What do you want?" he asked her harshly.

She blushed, but she held her ground.

"Not you," she returned pleasantly.

He gave her a rather haughty look and frowned. "What do you mean?"

Camilla gave him a nice sunny smile and refused to answer him directly. Instead she turned rather pointedly to me.

"Suki darling, Gideon says we're to make the most of the celebrations tonight and that he's coming with us to make sure that we do!" She turned almost reluctantly to Joseph. "I suppose you can come too, if you really want to and if you're not too busy sulking!"

"I? *Sulk?*" he demanded indignantly.

"Of course you're sulking! You've sulked solidly ever since you got back from Delhi!" She sat down beside me, hunching up her shoulders to add point to what she was saying. "You know what," she went on, "I should have thought it was a great deal easier to do your work than to worry about the results of not doing it! It's only an opinion, of course," she added hastily.

I had some difficulty in refraining from laughing. Joseph looked like a thundercloud and almost as young as Camilla. It came as a shock to me to realise that I could sit back and watch the two of them and feel the next best thing to old and experienced!

"And what do you know about it?" Joseph mocked her, but he was visibly shaken all the same. "You don't have to do anything at all all day!"

"I find myself enough to keep occupied," she answered smugly. "How about you?"

Joseph flushed angrily.

"I don't know what's the matter with me," he complained. "I don't seem to be able to please anyone today."

Camilla looked fleetingly sympathetic, but it didn't last long.

"Perhaps you don't try hard enough?" she suggested.

But Joseph had had enough. He glared at her and then at me and then silently took himself off, his hands in his pockets and scuffing the toes of his shoes as if he more than half expected us to call him back. Camilla looked sadly after him.

"What's the matter with him?" she asked impatiently. "Doesn't he know that it hurts when he goes into a grouch?"

I looked at her closely, noticing the drooping lips and the tears in the corners of her eyes. She looked the picture of heartache bravely borne, and I felt terribly sorry for her.

"I don't suppose he thinks," I answered. "Does it really matter to you?"

She closed her eyes and the tears squeezed out on to her cheeks. Restlessly, she wiped them away with the back of her hand.

"Yes," she admitted. "It matters very much."

I felt a hollow sensation in my middle. I could remember only too clearly Gideon's admonition that Joseph was incapable of being friends with any woman. It was only now that I was beginning to see what he meant.

"The trouble is," I began, "that men don't grow up nearly as quickly as we do. Joe is all right, but he doesn't really know where he's going."

Camilla began to cry in earnest, the tears spilling out of her eyes with increasing ease.

"But I'm young too!" she cried out. "And he isn't even interested!"

I sighed, knowing that I was going to have to talk about Timothy and not really wanting to, because he was still so recent in my own past that the scars could hurt a little, when I thought about it, which hadn't been often these last few days.

"You see," I said, "Joseph is just like Timothy, so I feel I know him rather well."

Camilla stopped crying immediately and gazed at me in astonishment.

"Your *Timothy*?"

I smiled wryly. "Yes, my Timothy. Why not?"

"Well, I don't know," she said uncomfortably. "Gideon said I wasn't to ask you about him, though we were both dying with curiosity," she added naïvely.

For an instant I was shocked that they should have discussed me, not because I was afraid of anything that either of them might have said, but simply because I shouldn't have thought that I was an interesting enough topic for their speculations.

"Both of you?" I asked dryly. "I can't believe that Gideon was much interested?"

"Oh, but you're wrong!" Camilla insisted. "He said Timothy didn't sound your sort at all. Oh, do tell me about him, Suki. Was he madly attractive?"

I blushed a little.

"No, he was quite ordinary. He was very clever and he suffered agonies with his digestion. It was important to see that he ate the right things and things like that!"

A look of distaste crossed Camilla's features.

"And were you really in love with him?" she asked.

"I suppose so," I said softly. I was horribly aware that I had just been discussing him in the past tense as if he were dead and I felt guilty. When we had parted we had parted only for two years—not for life!

"I don't think you were," Camilla said practically.

"He was just an interest for you. I expect you needed something while you were studying."

I gazed at her with respect. And to think that I had started out in this conversation to warn her of the dangers of youthful infatuation!

"Well, yes," I admitted. "Like Joseph."

She smiled a rather superior smile and she didn't look young at all.

"And that's why you think they are alike, Timothy and Joseph?" she asked me.

I nodded. It *was* why they were alike. They were both cast in the same mould, lovable but weak, not the sort of man I really wanted at all.

"It's difficult to admit," I went on with decision, "but I've grown out of Timothy. It happens that way sometimes. No matter how much you think you are in love with a person, you change and so do they, and you find you are no longer in love with them at all."

Camilla smiled more broadly.

"And you think that's what will happen to what I feel for Joseph?"

"Well, yes," I said very gently because I didn't want to hurt her. "You see Joseph isn't very mature, is he?"

Camilla shook her head at me.

"You don't really understand at all," she told me. "Timothy was one thing and of course you feel differently out here about him. Gideon says he doesn't believe you were ever in love with him at all! But what I feel for Joe is quite different! You see I know he's silly and weak and a bit lazy, but it doesn't make any *difference* to me."

I tried hard to think back to what I had thought about Timothy. It was surprisingly difficult. It had been a mixture of hero-worship and a fear that I would displease him, I thought. He had been there always, persuading me that I was cleverer than I really was by making clever remarks that I couldn't really understand but would have died rather than have admitted it. And

I had felt maternally concerned about him plying him with stomach powders and overseeing his diet like some fussy mother hen. No, I was quite sure now that I had never been in love with Timothy Black.

"I don't see what it has to do with Gideon," I said with a throat that had suddenly gone dry.

Camilla grinned.

"Poor Suki!" she murmured. "You know, of the two of us, you're the poor mixed-up kid! And don't for heaven's sake start worrying about Joseph and me! We'll look after each other perfectly well. *You'd* do better to worry about Julie!"

"Why?" I asked blankly.

Her face filled with impatience mixed with despair.

"If you don't know, *I'm* not going to tell you!" she exclaimed, and sauntered off into the house to find out what had happened to dinner. I stood up myself and stared out into the darkness. Here and there a firework burst forth, let loose by someone's impatient fingers. As an older woman and a confidante, I had not been a howling success, I thought, and for some reason I could have cried.

Gideon joined us for dinner. With a great deal of laughter he had fashioned for himself a couple of crutches, tipping them with pieces of an old tyre he had cut up so that they wouldn't slip on the floors. He came across the verandah with a flourish of independence and a broad grin on his face.

"Isn't that something?" he demanded.

I laughed. "That's something!" I agreed.

He sat down heavily and chuckled.

"Know something, you're getting quite cheeky!" he teased me. "How does it feel to have a whole village *en fête* for you?"

"Unbelievable!" I told him. "Not that it is for me exactly. I think they're really beginning to realise what this dam could mean to them."

His eyes twinkled. "Well, the dam is your project!" He laughed at my discomfiture. "And a hell of a lot of work you're going to find it! Have they done their full day's quota?"

I shook my head. "No, but this is the first day. It'll take a day or so to make it clear exactly what has to be done. I'm hoping then it'll go like a bomb, as Joe would say."

The smile died out of Gideon's eyes.

"What do you think of that young man?" he asked abruptly. "Did I hear you and Camilla talking about him earlier?"

I blushed to the ears, wondering what else he had heard.

"It was just in passing," I said.

He looked straight into my eyes. "Have you heard from that Timothy of yours recently?" he asked.

"No, I haven't, though I can't see what business it is of yours!" I added hotly.

He grinned. "I suppose you can't, you ridiculous blockhead! Don't you think it's about time you wrote to him?"

I wondered how he knew that I had put off writing because I had found that I hadn't anything much to say. To talk of my work would have bored Timothy, and to have talked of anything else would only have shown him pointedly how very well I was managing without him.

"I'll think about it!" I said lightly.

"Yes, do," he said. "The sooner you're free of that entanglement the better!"

But I wasn't sure that I saw it that way. Timothy, after all, was a form of defence. He wasn't a very good one, but he was the only one I had got. And at that moment I needed a defence very badly against the charms of Gideon Wait.

"I'm not sure I want to be free," I said stubbornly.

Gideon looked exasperated. "Muddle-headed and ridiculous!" he commented.

"I'm very fond of Timothy," I insisted.

Gideon blew up like a geyser. It was fascinating to see. Whoever would have thought that he held his temper on so light a rein? But he said nothing. He buried his head in his hands and groaned. Then: "Have it your own way," he said at last. "But don't be surprised if someone takes the trouble to wring your neck for you!"

From somewhere I found the audacity to laugh.

"Oh, really!" I protested weakly.

"Yes, really!" he told me.

Dinner passed in a whirl. I puzzled over what Gideon had said, but I couldn't see any good reason why he should care whether I wrote to Timothy or not. At last, when it was all over, I made my escape to my room and sat on the edge of my bed and tried to pull myself together. Outside the crowd was becoming noisier and noisier and the zip of the fireworks more frequent. The celebrations had officially begun.

The village was indeed *en fête*. I had only the haziest notion of what was going on, because the myths and legends of India must be almost as numerous as her extensive population. So who the two giants, stuffed with fireworks and explosive bangs, were remained a mystery, though I cheered as hard as any when they went up in smoke, in one uproarious spectacle of flare and colour, finally bursting into flames.

I recognised the King of the Monkeys, very much the noble ally, with his breast flapping in the breeze to reveal Rama's name written on his heart. But this demi-god, this humanised ape, bore little resemblance to the mischievous monkeys that had frightened me in the forest. I was disappointed when he too didn't burst into flames, but contented himself with throwing coloured water at all the pretty girls instead. Lakshmi was soaked in a glowing scarlet and I, to my intense annoyance, ended up multi-coloured like a patchwork quilt. It was all great fun, though, for the villagers, who knew little about fun and a great deal about grinding poverty. For a night they forgot that the uncertain monsoon was still a month away and they became men of substance with a high purpose in life, and their laughter and shrieks of merriment rang through the dusty street and into the deaf ears of the village goddess, now smelling more rancid than ever.

Some time during the evening Hanuman, the King of the Monkeys, lost the head of his disguise and I saw Lakshmi clinging to his arm as they ran through the crowds. So that was the way the land lay, I thought, and I hoped that her family were thinking along the same lines.

I was standing in the middle of the street, watching her, when Gideon came up behind me.

"All alone?" he asked.

I turned quickly. "Why, yes," I admitted. "But I don't mind. It's so colourful that one would almost spoil it all by talking."

"Is that a hint?"

I was afraid I had hurt his feelings.

"Of course not! Are you all alone too?"

"At the moment, but not for very long!" He could scarcely hide his contented grin.

I waited for him to tell me what was happening and when, but he didn't. He stood there, propped up on his crutches, and grinned straight into my face.

"You look very pleased about it anyway," I said crossly.

"I am," he chortled. "Julie is coming to stay at the end of the week!"

I could feel my face tightening into a social smile and my eyes go blank. The last thing I wanted was for him to know what I was really thinking and feeling. *That* would have been disastrous!

"Coming here?" I said hollowly.

He looked quite unbelievably pleased with himself.

"At my express invitation!" he announced proudly. "She'll have to shack down with you and Camilla in the small house, but she's very adaptable."

I thought of that cloud of mauve hair having to be dressed and touched up every week, and wondered.

"There isn't any room. There only are two bedrooms."

His grin appeared again, not one whit put out.

"Yes, I know," he said, "but Camilla says she doesn't mind doubling up with you for a week or so—"

"Or so?" I repeated faintly.

His eyes twinkled mercilessly.

"Oh, come now," he said, "I know you two girls blame the whole Burnett family for my accident, but it really had nothing at all to do with Julie—"

"Even if her father did trip you up?" I put in pugnaciously.

"It still wasn't her fault," he went on reasonably. "She was very upset and wept on my shoulder to show just how sorry she was. It will do her a lot of good to see exactly how and where I work. It isn't the same when she comes over for the day, because nobody does anything very much on those days, we're all so busy entertaining her."

"Exactly!" I said bleakly. "Now nobody will do anything for a week or so!"

He laughed out loud.

"Don't be silly!" he said. "With the monsoon only a month away we'll all be working flat out. Julie quite understands that. She won't get in your way at all, so don't look so worried!"

I gave him a look that was meant to put him in his place, but it seemed that nothing was going to wipe that smile off his face.

"I'll *bet* Camilla was pleased!" I said viciously.

"As a matter of fact she was—quite," he retorted.

But I didn't believe him! For who in their senses would want to welcome Julie Burnett into their house? It just didn't seem possible!

The feverish pleasure of the evening was beginning to die down. The old men had gathered beside the well, smoking and yarning to each other. Even the oldest of them was able to squat for hours without the slightest fatigue. In India people queued for buses that way, had their hair cut, mended their fishing nets, and they found it as natural as the European does to sit on a chair. But somehow the presence of the old men put a restraint on the younger villagers and their entertainments that were rapidly turning into mobilised hysteria. The young men dropped the hands of veiled young girls and returned to the pretence that they didn't know them or anything about them. I looked around for Lakshmi, but she was nowhere to be seen. Everyone was tired and happy and they smiled as Gideon and I went slowly up the street, I waiting every few steps for him to manipulate his crutches on the uneven surface of the road.

"Well, your dam has been well and truly sent off," Gideon observed. "I hope we can live up to their expectations."

I could have hugged him for taking some of the responsibility on to his own shoulders. I had worried all I knew in case the rains came before we were ready, and the mere fact that someone else was with me in the venture made it all seem more likely to succeed.

"If they'll dig—" I began.

"They'll dig if you get out among them and keep them going," he said.

I nodded seriously. "That's what I intend to do," I said.

The old men called Gideon over to join them. He hitched himself on to the edge of the well and put his crutches thankfully down on the ground. When he had done, he patted the ledge beside him, inviting me to sit down beside him, but I shook my head. The old men were well launched on their stories and they wouldn't have wanted a woman to sit among them. Instead, I walked back down the street and gathered some of the lost coloured streamers into my hands as a memento of the evening. The whole air smelt of joss-sticks and gunpowder and the flat, spicy smell that permeates all India. If Julie hadn't been coming, it would have been the end of a perfect evening.

Camilla was already undressing when I got back to the small house that we shared between us.

"Have you seen Lakshmi?" she called out to me.

"Not recently," I replied.

Camilla appeared in the doorway of her room, clad in no more than a light chiffon robe.

"That's the trouble with this country," she said. "One can't do anything by oneself. I thought I'd have a bath, but if Lakshmi isn't here who will scrub my back for me?"

I laughed.

"I will if you like," I offered, knowing that it involved a great deal more than that. It was a question of finding the bath and heating the water.

"Have you really got the time?" Camilla asked me. "It's terribly late!"

"Never mind. It will be soothing after all those hectic crowds," I said.

She giggled and padded back into her room, leaving the door open for me to follow her.

"I'll go and raise the bath," she began.

I took one look at her and pushed her farther into the room.

"Not like that! I'll go and get the bath and arrange for some hot water. You can be thinking of a good story to explain away your sudden enthusiasm for Julie!"

She sat on the edge of her bed with her mouth half open and a look of consternation on her face.

"But it wasn't like that—" she started to assure me.

"Oh, wasn't it?" I said grimly, and I set off for the bath, slamming the door behind me.

Lakshmi still hadn't come in when the water was boiling happily and I had dragged the bath down the corridor to Camilla's room. She pulled it inside and set it down on the floor while I went back for the first lot of water.

"Whatever makes you think *I* want Julie here?" she demanded when I returned.

"Your brother! He told me quite positively that you didn't mind doubling up with me for a week or so!"

"Well, no more I should!" she said, still puzzled.

"So that *Julie* can have your room?"

"Certainly not! What is all this about Julie?"

I swooshed the hot water into the bath with such energy that it very nearly went over the edge on the opposite side.

"Gideon has invited Julie *here*. He thinks it will do her a lot of good to see the sort of conditions that he works under. Besides," I added maliciously, "she's very upset!"

From the look on her face it was easy to see that Camilla shared my revulsion.

"He couldn't *want* her here!" she said faintly.

"He seems to," I said bluntly.

She shook her head. "I just don't believe it! I'm sure he has some ulterior motive and is just not telling us." She giggled suddenly. "I'm not at all sure that I can't guess what it is!" she exclaimed.

I helped her into the bath and poured some water down her back.

"Aren't you going to share the joke?" I asked with some asperity.

She looked round at me, her eyes alight with mischievous laughter.

"No, I'm not," she said. "You wouldn't appreciate it anyway!"

With some difficulty I recovered my good humour and doused her with a spongeful of water.

"Oh, wouldn't I?" I said. "And why not, please?"

But she only shook her head.

"I think I'll ask Joseph what he thinks," she said.

It took time to finish the bath to Camilla's satisfaction. She liked a cloud of bath-salts followed by a cloud of talcum powder and she had no intention of being cheated out of either.

"It takes time to soak the heat out of your skin," she complained when I tried to hurry her out of the water. "Why don't you come in after me?"

I was tempted, but it was already terribly late.

"If you come out right now!"

"Oh, all right!" She stood up and accepted the towel that I offered her, drying herself efficiently and with great speed, hopping into bed and under the single sheet that was all the bed proffered.

I went along to my own room to collect my night things and when I came back Lakshmi was there.

"Will I bring you more water?" she asked. Her eyes never quite reached mine and she looked suddenly shy.

"Why, Lakshmi," I said, "it's happened, hasn't it?"

She nodded. "It is very bad! My family will never agree!"

I sat on the end of Camilla's bed and she squarked as she guarded her feet from me.

"Isn't the King of the Monkeys good enough?" I asked.

Lakshmi giggled. "You saw me!" she accused.

"Uh-huh!" I teased her. "Was it to be a big secret?"

Camilla looked from one to the other of us. "Lakshmi has fallen in love!" she concluded. "Oh, how lovely! Tell us all about it, Lakshmi. Is he tall and brave and handsome?"

Lakshmi giggled again. "That's all you think about, Miss Camilla!" She sighed. "But yes, he is very beautiful. As Krishna must have been when he walked the earth. He has the softest eyes!"

"Who was Krishna?" Camilla asked.

"One of the gods," I told her. "He was a great one with the women!"

Lakshmi frowned. "Who is human and who is divine?" she asked in a puzzled voice. "All I know is that he is beautiful."

Camilla watched her with eyes gone soft. "I know what you mean," she said. "And I can tell you that I'm strictly human when Joseph is around."

"Camilla!" I exclaimed.

"Oh, nuts! *I* know what I mean!"

"I wish I didn't!" I said, putting on my most disapproving face.

The bath was almost cold by the time I got into it. Lakshmi fussed around offering to bring more water, but she looked so sad and tired that I felt I would have been imposing on her.

"Don't worry, Lakshmi," I said, when I had finished drying myself and was gathering up my things to go back to my own room. "I'll tell the *Sahib* Wait all about it in the morning. He'll probably be able to sort it all out for you."

Lakshmi's weariness fell away from her with a rush and her dark eyes gleamed with excitement.

"Do you think so? It would be so wonderful! The *Sahib* knows all my family, so perhaps he could persuade them. But I'm not important enough to bother him— Do you think he really would?"

Camilla pulled the sheet more closely around her shoulders.

"Of course he'll help," she said sleepily. "He's my brother, isn't he?"

It was no longer night proper when I went back to my own room, it was already the early hours of the morning. If I were sensible, I thought, I would make the most of the few remaining hours of darkness and get some sleep. It was going to be a long, hard day and I knew it, and yet I couldn't go to sleep yet. When I shut my eyes the fireworks zipped and zooped once more and the smell of gunpowder and the spicy odour of curry assailed my nostrils, mixed with marigolds and rancid butter. It was something to write and tell Timothy about, I thought suddenly. Something to show him that I was making a life for myself without him, that I didn't give a rap.

I got out of bed and found pen and paper and started my letter. It was all so easy once I had begun. It was no trouble at all to tell him that I didn't want two years of waiting, that I wanted to be free. I knew perfectly well that he wouldn't care, on the contrary he would only be mildly relieved to know that at last I had come to my senses and knew finally that we were not made for each other.

I finished the letter, sealed it and affixed the stamp. It was only then that I realised that I had done exactly what Gideon had told me to do. I had written to Timothy.

CHAPTER ELEVEN

THE digging went on at a great rate. I spent most of my time out there with them, trying to ignore the frantic heat, and to do my share of breaking up the concrete-hard surface of the earth. The sun burned my skin a dark brown until I was almost as dark as Lakshmi. Joseph made several teasing references to the dark beauty who had suddenly come among them, but as everybody knew that I was not in the least lovely to look at, they fell rather flat. Camilla, with far more subtlety than I should have expected from her, began a systematic campaign to divert Joseph's attention to herself. Sometimes I wondered if Gideon knew, or had even noticed, but I was far too tired and full of heat and sun to do anything about it. Besides, Camilla often seemed far more capable of looking after herself than I should ever be, so I buried myself in my work and let the world pass by me.

Until Julie came.

It began as a day like any other. I didn't see Gideon at breakfast because I had taken to having my own as early as possible to get as much done before the crushing heat of midday as was possible. In fact I had very nearly forgotten that Julie was coming and what with having so much to do it had become almost unimportant to me. It was probably because of that that it seemed all the more of a shock when I came in to lunch and found her sitting on the verandah, an expanse of neatly stockinged leg stretched out before her and looking unbelievably cool and pretty in her symphony of blues.

Camilla made a face at me behind her back and I gathered that she was not being a very easy guest as far as she was concerned, but I was too weary to care. I flung myself into the nearest chair and stared moodily out at the sun.

"How long before it rains, do you think?"

Joseph laughed.

"You don't have to mind her, Julie! She asks the same question every day at lunchtime. The trouble is that she's obsessed by this dam of hers."

"So would you be, if you were breaking your back on that ground out there!" I grumbled good-naturedly.

"And how you'd hate it if he were!" Camilla put in. "Perhaps Julie would like to help you while she's here?" she added with deliberate malice.

Julie shook her head, summoning up a smile.

"I don't think I should be any help at all!" she said hastily. "Why, dear, I hardly recognised you! You're burned to a crisp!"

"Yes, I know," I said wearily. "I'm hoping to return to normal when the rains come."

Julie's eyes widened with memory.

"Oh, but you don't know what it's like *then*," she said. "Oozing mud and *inches* of rain every day. Even my parents long for the green fields of England during the monsoons!"

Gideon had practically mastered walking with his home-made crutches, I noticed, as he came down the verandah towards us. He grinned at Julie and gave her a downright affectionate look.

"Settled in?" he asked her.

She fussed herself and her chair out of his way and oversaw his lowering himself down into one of the chairs with careful solicitude.

"Oh yes, I'm completely comfortable!" she sighed. "I brought some of my things with me, so that the room wouldn't be too bare, you know, and they look just lovely here!"

Camilla giggled and choked. Gideon gave her a severe

look, but nothing could muffle her complete glee over Julie's possessions.

"What sort of things did you bring?" I asked.

She coloured prettily, turning the palest shade of coral.

"Well, you know I'm not *tough* like you," she said, making me feel like the strong woman of some circus. "I couldn't possibly sleep on one of those *charpoys,* so I had to bring a bed with me, didn't I?"

"I suppose so," I agreed, a gurgle beginning at the back of my own throat.

Gideon frowned at me. He put out a hand and patted Julie's consolingly.

"Nobody would expect you to sleep on a bed of nails," he teased her gently.

"Certainly not!" I added dryly. I was surprised by the quick flash of amusement in Gideon's eyes, equally quickly suppressed.

I went off hastily to wash my hands before I succumbed to open laughter too and, like Joseph and Camilla, openly derided Gideon's most feminine guest. It was a temptation that had to be overcome because somehow I had to show Gideon that I didn't care who he invited here.

When I saw my room most of my resolution failed me, however. It was piled high with suitcases and household furniture. And, sure enough, a brand new bed had been imported and was taking up most of the space in the centre of the room. An apologetic Lakshmi came running as soon as she heard my footsteps and came to an abrupt halt in the doorway.

"I thought Camilla was moving in with me," I said bitterly.

Lakshmi's wide eyes rested on mine for a second.

"This room is bigger," she explained.

"Ridiculous!" I exploded. "Have you ever seen anything like it?"

She said nothing, and after a while my anger changed

to laughter as I thought just how ridiculous the whole situation was.

"You'd better get my bed moved out to give her some more room!" I said weakly, and was rewarded by a quick giggle.

"I have already taken all your clothes and things," she told me apologetically. "There was no room to leave them here."

"None at all!" I agreed. It came as a wrench to leave that room, though. I had grown fond of its bleak bareness and the way it had refused to respond to the few bits and bobs that I had brought with me. Looking round it now it already looked quite different. A mass of photographs of the Burnett family littered the windowsills, and *her* clothes, quite different from mine with their frills and furbelows, were already draped across every available space.

Camilla's room, on the contrary, was almost as spartan as my own had been and only my own things, hastily moved down the corridor and not yet put away, were out of place. I washed my hands in the bowl on her washstand, flicking the cold water on to my sun-tanned face to cool myself down. I was just drying myself when Camilla came in and flung herself down on her bed.

"Don't blame me!" she began. "How can Gideon tolerate her?"

"She's very feminine," I said repressively.

Camilla sat up and looked at me. Her eyes were as old as the wisdom of the world. She is growing up too fast, I thought, and wondered what I ought to do about it.

"Julie? Feminine?" she asked scornfully. "She's all promise and very little fulfilment, if you ask me! If Gideon were to kiss her, really kiss her, she'd die of fright!"

I laughed and felt a good deal better.

"You know, Camilla," I said, "there are times when I like you very much!"

She grinned. "I know!" she said. "But then you're in love with Gideon yourself!"

I could feel the blush burning up my cheeks to my hairline.

"Well, what if I am?" I demanded in prickly tones.

She got off the bed and hugged me.

"Nothing, I'm really very glad about it. You see, I can't help thinking you'd make a nicer sister-in-law than Julie Burnett!"

"*That* wouldn't be very difficult!" I said sourly.

"No," she agreed. "If only Gideon could see it!"

But Gideon seemed determined to be as blind as a bat as far as I was concerned. At lunch he scarcely said a dozen words to me. But perhaps he didn't have much opportunity, because Julie talked nineteen to the dozen all through the meal, telling us all about her stay in Delhi. There was no doubt but that she had had a very good time there, and I spent most of lunch thinking how nice it would have been if she had stayed there.

The long chain of home-made buckets hesitated and then came to a halt at a signal from the foreman. The men threw down the buckets where they stood and went over to the bank they were creating to lounge in the pitiful bit of shade it provided. One of the older men had brought his *sitar*, a whining and much-loved musical instrument, with him and he started plucking at the strings, catching at a melody here and there to see if anyone would join in one of the ancient and endless songs they all loved so well. There must have been a similar scene at the building of the Taj Mahal or any other monument or mud-hut throughout India. The workers, their clothes the same colour as the dust around them; the richer among them with their midday meal done up in a cloth that had long ago been faded to the same dun colour by the fierce sun; the same separation of the different castes and religions, but the same unity of purpose that had already moved tons and tons of earth to build my dam.

I sat on the bank beside them wondering if the reservoirs were going to be big enough to hold the tremendous volume of water that would be necessary for the needs of the village all through the dry season when the evaporation would be at its height. I wished I were a proper engineer, but it was obvious that any water would be better than none and so I knew that even the small amount that we were doing would transform the local crops.

"We're almost ready for the P.V.C.," Joseph commented from his perch above me. "When's it coming?"

"Any time now," I replied. "Gideon received the dispatching order some days ago."

Joseph grunted.

"It's probably down at the station waiting for someone to go and collect it. I'll take the jeep down and make some enquiries."

"Oh, would you?" I was pleased that he was taking an interest. "Why don't you take Camilla with you?"

"How about my own true love?" he asked.

I frowned repressively. "I have work to do here," I said. "And anyway, why do you have to use such facetious expressions?"

He shrugged. "Ever thought that they might be true?"

"Never!" I said firmly. "Please hurry, Joe. I'll need that stuff this afternoon. The welder too. They promised to send it at the same time, so make sure that it's come, won't you?"

"I can be trusted to do *some* things right!" he grinned at me.

I grinned right back at him. "Yes, I know. Camilla knows it too," I added, and then wished I hadn't. Camilla was so very young still, and what would Gideon say if he knew I was encouraging her friendship with Joseph?

Joseph only looked puzzled, however.

"Does she though?" he said. "May I take your jeep?"

I gave my consent easily enough, though I did wonder what had gone wrong with his own this time. For a mechanic, Joseph was surprisingly haphazard when it came to the combustion engine, but then who was I to complain? After the first day he had kept mine going for me and it went well, I had to admit that.

When he had gone, I went down into the bottom of the reservoir to make sure that no stones had been left that would gash the P.V.C. and spoil its waterproofing qualities. Some of the older men were raking the loose earth into patterns that formed symbols of good luck. On some days, they told me, on feast days, their women raked the floors of their houses in the same way, making patterns to please the gods. A youth with the only wheel-barrow—the rest of the men carried everything by hand in their home-made buckets—came trundling by, lethargically picking up the heaviest of the rocks as they were pulled free from the dusty earth. He went off again, jauntily keeping in time with the chanted beat of the rest of the men.

When I came back to the bank Julie had come out in Gideon's jeep to have a look round. I saw her pale mauve fluffy hair and the vivid cerise of her dress from quite a distance, and I am ashamed to say I spent the whole way over to her half looking for an excuse to break away and go off in some other direction.

"Hullo," she said as I plodded up the bank towards her. She looked cool and her face had the well-powdered look that I had long ago despaired of. By way of contrast I knew quite well that my own face was shiny with sweat and my clothes rumpled and sadly stained by the dusty soil.

"Hullo," I replied a trifle cagily. "What do you think of my pet project?"

"It looks—expensive," she said. "I suppose it has meant delaying quite a lot of other things?"

"I suppose it did," I agreed, surprised by her real interest. "It will be worth it, though. We badly need this water."

She smiled faintly. "Worth it to you, don't you mean?"

"Well, yes," I said, frankly puzzled.

She smiled again. "What I mean is that Gideon doesn't get anything out of it? I imagine all the credit goes down under your name?"

I laughed, relieved that I had caught on to her meaning.

"Oh, we don't work like that!" I told her. "Gideon is running the station, so of course he'll get a lot of the credit—a lot of the blame too if it doesn't work, come to that!"

Julie got out of the jeep, looking really anxious.

"There isn't any chance of that, surely?" she demanded.

I looked round the gigantic earthworks that I had somehow caused to be dug in the dust, away in the middle of nowhere. It seemed a greater gamble at that moment than it had ever seemed. I ran a dusty hand across my hot brow, adding a smear to my already far from clean face.

"It's a distinct possibility," I said. "I'm not an engineer, you know."

She lifted her elegant eyebrows and stared at me out of her blue eyes.

"You mean you started all this without knowing anything about it at all!"

"Pretty well," I admitted. "I've seen it done at home in England, but the problems aren't quite the same."

"Look," she said, brushing away my remark. "I want

to talk to you. Does anyone around here speak English?"

I shrugged my shoulders. "Some do."

She pouted, patting her skirt into place around her slim hips.

"Never mind, it'll have to do. Gideon doesn't seem to get out much with his leg in plaster, so we never have an opportunity back at the house, do we?"

I sat down on the bank and wished that Joseph would come back with the P.V.C. The sky looked very odd to me and I was getting increasingly fearful that the rains would come before we were ready.

"Do you think it will rain this week?" I asked pessimistically.

Julie made a gesture of impatience.

"Who cares? Susan, I may call you Susan, mayn't I?"

"Most people call me Suki," I told her carelessly.

"How quaint! Not that it matters. What are you going to do when you've finished this dam?"

My enthusiasm was immediately aroused.

"But don't you see? Once we have water we can really get to work! I hope to double or even treble most of the crops in my charge. It will take more than water, of course. Selective breeding, proper manures and modern methods will make a tremendous difference too. It's exciting, don't you think?"

Julie tossed her head and I was pleased to see that she also was beginning to feel the heat. She was not a super-woman after all.

"I'm afraid it wouldn't excite me," she said primly. "I think it's rather a masculine interest for a woman."

So we were back on that again! But this time I felt more sorry for her than angry.

"Didn't you ever want to do something rather than stay at home?" I asked impulsively.

She gave me a cynical smile.

"Oh, I think you have to be rather insecure to want

to compete with men in their own fields. My father has always given me everything I want. Why should I want to work myself? All I want to do is marry and be a good wife."

I swallowed down my impatience with the whole Burnett family.

"Here, in India?" I asked her.

She leaned against the jeep with a secret look in her eyes.

"It will have to be in India," she said. "I can't imagine England would suit me at all! Servants at a premium and those cold winters! Besides, Gideon has rather turned his back on England, hasn't he?"

I wiped the sweat out of my eyes and looked at her.

"Not necessarily," I told her. "He might go back any time and work there if an interesting opportunity arose."

She bit her lip and trembled, her champagne hair nodding in the wind.

"I'm telling you! He can't go back to England! My parents are here and they would never leave, so you see—" Her voice trailed away and she smiled. "But I forgot," she said. "You don't like my parents, do you?"

"No," I said briefly, "I don't."

"Charming!" she retorted. "Not that it matters. *You* will be going back to England."

"Oh? Is that a threat or a promise?"

She tossed her head. She looked very sure of herself, but then perhaps she had reason. Gideon had asked her to stay, after all.

"It was advice really. Camilla will be going back to England soon. If you're wise, you'll go with her. There isn't room here for us both, is there?"

"We'll see," I answered. The rains had not yet come and Gideon was still a free man. But I couldn't bear to look at her again in case she knew how she had unsettled me. And I didn't want her to know that I too was in love with Gideon and that unless I was terribly firm with myself I went soft inside at the mere thought of him, and *that* knowledge I didn't want to share with anyone at all!

Julie smiled gently into the distance.

"No, we shan't see at all," she said. "I'm telling you!"

That rather brought the conversation to a close, and I think my relief must have been more than obvious when Joseph came triumphantly back from the railway with the news that the P.V.C. had arrived. He drove the jeep straight up the bank and practically into the reservoir. With a paralysing whoop, Camilla jumped clear and landed in a huddle beside us.

"Are you all right?" I asked her, laughing.

She jumped to her feet, sheer exuberance in living showing in her every movement. Then her eyes fell on Julie and her smile died.

"What are you doing here?" she demanded rudely.

Julie looked at the young girl, noting the dust on her hair and the creases of her face.

"What are you doing, dear?" she returned coldly. "I'm sure Gideon would never approve if he knew you were holding up the great work!"

I interrupted quickly before Camilla could say anything which she might later regret.

"What nonsense! She and Joseph have just been to collect the P.V.C. Where is it, by the way?"

"It's following," Joseph shouted to me triumphantly. He leaned out of the jeep and pulled Camilla back into the seat beside him. "Gideon wants to know when you start welding and he'll be out to help."

A tide of excitement rose within me.

"Tell him I'll be waiting for him," I answered cheerfully.

Joe backed the jeep off down the slope, practically turning it over at the bottom, he was going at such a speed. I grinned and waved at the two of them and then turned my attention back to Julie. To my surprise her face was taut with temper.

"How dare he just ignore me?" she demanded. "How dare he?"

I said nothing. It didn't seem to matter what she said just then. The P.V.C. had arrived at just the right moment and Gideon was coming to help to lay it.

It was a very long job. The sheets of P.V.C. were laid out, edge to edge, until they covered the whole of the dug-out area. Anxiously, I helped to walk out the air pockets underneath before we welded the edges together to form a single bottom to the gigantic tank.

"Right," I said at last. "We can begin welding."

We sat on the bank and waited for Gideon. He came almost immediately. He had come to terms with his leg now and could manage quite well despite the heavy plaster that destroyed his natural balance and made movement so awkward. He came towards us, dragging his leg, but otherwise unperturbed by it.

"Is it as hot out here as you look?" he asked me.

I wiped the perspiration away from my brow almost resentfully.

"It's extremely hot!" I retorted. "I daresay one can stay cool with nothing to do but sit on the verandah—" His grin brought me to an abrupt halt.

"I hope you're not referring to me," he said quite gently.

But I refused to answer. He was in love with Julie and I would do well to remember it. Instead I turned away, looking in the jeep for the welder, but Joseph had already taken it out on to the reservoir. Shyly, I glanced up at Gideon to find he was still smiling, so I grasped him by the hand and pulled him down the slope and on to the P.V.C. bottom. It was black and shiny, reflecting the sun into our faces. Gideon stopped and bent down to touch it.

"Hmm," he said thoughtfully. "It should keep the water in. What else are you going to do with it?"

I explained that I had thought to cover it with a few

inches of soil so that it would not be perished in the strong rays of the sun.

"Fair enough," he nodded. "I can see that by this time next year we shall be sitting on the banks and fishing in the waters."

"Oh, do you really think so?" I asked enthusiastically. "It would be great fun!"

"I thought you'd think so," he said with satisfaction.

"If I'm still here," I added uncertainly.

He looked at me in surprise. "Of course you'll be here!" he said impatiently.

But I knew that I wouldn't be, not if Julie Burnett was to come instead.

We worked hard until it grew dark and the gangs of men began to think about lighting their fires and eating their scanty meal before bed. The ones who lived locally started back to the village on the collection of rusty bicycles that was their main form of transport anywhere. A few of the more devout began their evening prayers, the Moslems bowing down to Mecca, the Hindus fulfilling their own ritual. The air was filled with the scent of charcoal and burning cow-dung, mixed with the occasional joss-stick and the hot smell of curry. It was time to go home.

Gideon sat beside me in the jeep as I drove home. I was terribly conscious of him as I pressed the starter and navigated the vehicle through the clattering bicycles and the silent shapes that plodded through the gloom.

Gideon stretched his tired limbs and grunted.

"There may be disadvantages in employing females," he said comfortably, "but this is one of the big advantages!"

I held on to the wheel with one hand while I swatted at some insect with the other.

"What is?"

His smile was particularly charming in the dusky light.

"Why, travelling through the darkness with you, what else?"

It would have been bliss if I hadn't known that he was teasing me.

"You'd better let me concentrate on my driving, then," I said primly, "or it might not be such fun after all!"

He chuckled. "Are you planning to ditch me, Suki?"

I could feel myself blushing.

"I—I—" I began. "I haven't the foggiest idea what we're talking about!"

"No? You must be feeling very obtuse!"

I made an irate gesture and we very nearly left the dusty strip that passed as a road. With an effort I pulled at the wheel to find that Gideon's hand was already there. As soon as we were straight he placed his hand over mine and it was as much as I could do to steer at all.

"It isn't kind to play with other people's feelings!" I tossed at him.

His eyebrows shot up.

"Is that what I'm doing? How interesting! By the way, I've been meaning to tell you all afternoon that there's a letter waiting for you at the station."

"For me?" I stammered.

"That's right. A pale blue envelope with an American stamp on it!"

My mouth went suddenly dry. I put my foot on the accelerator and we shot forward. I braked very nearly as sharply and almost stalled the engine.

"Timothy," I whispered.

He grinned. "It seems likely, though if I'd known it was going to have this effect on you I would have waited until we got home before telling you about it!"

I apologised and concentrated harder on my driving.

"It isn't really very exciting," I tried to explain. "It's only the answer to my letter to him."

"So you did write?" he prompted me.

I nodded. "I don't suppose you'll ever understand," I said with a sudden burst of confidence. "I can't understand it myself! I was so sure that I was in love with Timothy!"

He turned off the ignition key and the jeep came slowly to a halt. For a second I thought my driving really had fallen to pieces, but I didn't really care. For the first time that day I felt cool and almost happy.

"What did you do that for?" I demanded.

He shrugged his shoulders.

"I just wanted to sit here for ever and watch the clouds blow overhead."

I looked up too at the sky. The clouds were long and dark, but I was sure that they would go overhead like all the others had done. I wasn't worried.

"Besides," Gideon went on, "I want to hear about your letter to Timothy."

I bit my lip, forgetting all about the clouds.

"There's nothing to tell," I said. "That's the trouble. There never was anything to tell, but I only realised it a week or so ago. I suddenly couldn't even remember his face properly!"

"Had you ever really looked at it?" he asked.

I was indignant, but I shook my head.

"I was far too busy prescribing his stomach powders!"

He laughed, and I found myself laughing too.

"Okay," he said. "Now that you've admitted that, you can drive us both home and read your letter."

I didn't want to move, but the memory of Julie didn't make me want to linger either.

"Do you think it will thunder?" I asked.

He put out his hands just as the first drops of rain began to descend from the sky.

"I think it's going to rain," he said, and we laughed like a couple of children. I only stopped laughing when I thought of all the welding that still had to be done.

CHAPTER TWELVE

I HAD never seen rain like it. By day I worked on the dam, the water dripping down the back of my neck. As soon as the welding of the P.V.C. was done, the men came behind carrying basketfuls of mud to cover the shiny black surface. Gideon, his leg so much better that they had pared away at the plaster until his movements were considerably less restricted, used the roller on the edges, weighting it down and rolling it into the soil until there was no chance of any of it breaking free and tearing. He and I both worked in boots, but the Indians didn't seem to care about any part of their body except their head. This was tenderly wrapped against both rain or any hint of a draught, as was only becoming in such an important member.

The narrow stream swelled into a river and the two tanks of the reservoir began to fill. The actual dam was not yet necessary and would have caused flooding, but everything was ready to control the flow of the water. At last, it seemed, the project was complete and there was no reason why the village should ever be short of water again.

And still it rained. Not the mild, caressing rain of the temperate lands, but it came pouring down, bouncing off the earth again and penetrating everywhere until the whole world was a sea of mud and steaming water.

"And to think that I thought the heat was trying!" I remarked one day to Camilla. We were both lying on our beds and despairing of the clamminess that we met with even in our own bodies and clothing.

Camilla sighed.

"It wouldn't be so bad if *she* would only go home!" she said mournfully.

I didn't trust myself to answer. The thought of Julie was a constant burden, weighing down my spirits and making me less and less sure of myself. She was like a cat in the rain, bad-tempered and spiteful, and she never went out if she could help it. It was only at night that she really came alive and she and Gideon would sit for hours on the verandah until the early hours of the morning. It had become impossible for me to sleep until I heard her high heels clattering down the corridor to what was now her room and the creak of the springs, grown rusty in the rain, as she got into the bed she had brought with her.

"Perhaps she never will go," I said thoughtlessly.

Camilla sat up with a bounce. "What do you mean?"

I got off the bed with decision. "Nothing! Gideon likes having her here, though, so why shouldn't she stay?"

"I could give you any number of reasons!" Camilla said flatly.

I ruffled through the papers that I had left on the table so that I would have to deal with them sooner or later, and came across Timothy's letter. How funny, I thought, that I had hardly bothered to read it that evening, I had been so taken up with what Gideon had had to say and so hopeful of so many things. I spread it out now and saw that the corners were covered with fine mould where it must have got wet at some time or another.

"I think she's mad, like her parents!" Camilla announced quite casually.

"Very likely!" I agreed.

Timothy's handwriting was practically incomprehensible, but I could make out sufficient words to get the gist of what he was saying. He was glad that I was happy in India because it was extremely unlikely that he would ever return to England. The work he was doing was interesting and, he thought, valuable to the

Western world. The Western world certainly seemed to think so, judging by the salary they were paying him. He was eating better too. The doctors had recommended that he live on a diet of milk, steaks and vitamin pills and he had never felt better. He thought he would probably marry in America and settle down there. If ever I wanted to visit he was sure that there were any number of people who would be willing to put me up for a few days, only he thought I would really be better off in India as I seemed to like it so much. He hadn't time to write any more, but he would send a card at Christmas with a picture of some rockets on it.

"Joseph says she simply hates you," Camilla told me with relish. "Lucky you, that's all I can say. She seems determined that we shall be bosom friends."

I laughed. "You're Gideon's sister," I said dryly.

She blinked determinedly at me.

"I wonder what she'll think when I marry Joe," she mused. "He says we have to wait until Gideon accepts that his work is as good as anyone else's, but that won't be for ever!"

I turned quickly. "But, Camilla, you're so young!"

Camilla hugged her knees happily. "All the better! I'll have all the more years with Joseph! Is that letter from your Timothy?"

I nodded sadly, because it was sad, in a way, that Timothy had never been mine and never would be.

"He says he'll send a card with some of his rockets on it for Christmas," I said rather bitterly. It wouldn't have been so bad if his rockets had been of any use, like—like taking Julie Burnett somewhere far away into outer space!

"And you *like* him?" Camilla demanded, wrinkling up her nose in displeasure.

"Not much," I admitted honestly. "But he was there, and now there's no one."

Camilla looked very wise and nodded her head.

"Never mind," she said. "You have the dam, and

now that it's finished—all but!—and the rains have come, it'll make you famous!"

Which was cold comfort indeed and not at all what I wanted. With my usual neat, precise movements, I tore Timothy's letter up into little pieces and threw them away in the waste-paper basket. One of the best things about a research station is that there is always work to be done and one can't feel sorry for oneself for long with a test-tube in one hand and a spade in the other. If I couldn't be loved at least I could be dedicated.

"Oh, by the way," Camilla added, "you don't really have to worry about Julie, because I have a plan to deal with her. I'm *not* having her for a sister-in-law, whatever she might think!"

I gazed at her helplessly.

"I don't think you ought to interfere," I said at last.

But Camilla was not so easily dissuaded.

"How many days is it until the last concrete block is placed on the dam? That will be when she decides to go, you'll see!"

I must say I hoped that Camilla was right, but it seemed very unlikely. Julie spread her possessions about the house, like a spider wrapping up its victim in its web. Nothing escaped her soft sweetness or her cloying endearments.

I met her on my way to the village to discuss with the old men our plans for working the dam when the monsoon finally came to an end.

"Are you going out again?" she asked me.

I smiled and nodded. "Have you seen Gideon?" I countered.

Her expression didn't change, but she became very still and watchful.

"He doesn't want to see you just now," she said at last. "He's busy with other things."

"I see," I said. "Perhaps you'd tell him that the rice needs weeding at the top of the valley?"

"I'll try to remember," she smiled. "Have you thought any more about going back to England?"

"Not yet." It was so difficult being pleasant to her when I wanted to throw her out of the house, to destroy the pretty image she lived behind and, absurdly, to find out what colour her hair really was when she didn't bleach it and colour it blue. I turned to look at her, lounging on one of the chairs on the verandah. "Would you like to walk down to the village with me? It isn't raining at the moment, for a change."

She retired into herself, looking small and rather pathetic.

"Oh no, I couldn't! The mud would ruin my shoes!" She smiled her secret smile. "I'm not tough like you," she added, her voice tinged with malice.

"No," I agreed comfortably, "you're not." And without waiting to see if the shot had gone home, I started off to the village.

In the few fine minutes between downpours of rain everybody had come outside to do their shopping and to gossip to their neighbours. I knew a great many of them by now, with their intricate relationships and strict divisions into caste. Lakshmi's sister came running across the street and touched my arm. We smiled and greeted one another and she went off giggling happily.

The gentlemen of the *panchayat* were waiting for me in the metalsmith's small shop. We went through the shop, with its shavings of copper, tin and other metals and that inimitable smell of hot metal, and into the living space behind where one of the more venerable of the old men lived. They were already seated cross-legged on the floor, while an old woman went from one to the other with a damp flannel so that they could wipe their hands before eating the sweetmeats she set before them. My host greeted me with gentle courtesy and I was surprised to see that Gideon was already seated beside him.

"You're late!" he said to me with a grin.

"I was waiting for it to stop raining," I explained. Try as I would I was quite incapable of sitting comfortably on the floor, but Gideon seemed to manage it, his broken leg sticking out in front of him, the other neatly folded into his groin just like any Indian.

The old men watched me settle myself, their intense excitement coming like waves from their bodies, until I became aware of it and wondered what had caused it.

"We have heard from the government," our host told me in tones pregnant with awed complacency. "They are coming to see our dam. They are coming to see for themselves what can be done to preserve water!"

I looked round their solemn faces and felt rather proud of our achievement myself. Gideon was grinning at me and I smiled back at him.

"When are they coming?" I asked.

The old men stroked their beards in renewed ecstasy.

"They are coming on the day of the new moon."

"Next Saturday," Gideon supplied. They all nodded, their eyes shining with excitement, and I was terribly glad that, for the moment at any rate, I was one of them. This was *my* village and I was extremely proud of it.

We were served with little curry sandwiches and Coca-Cola. The women half knelt, half sat on the floor, with their array of plates before them and served us by hand, carefully picking out a morsel to please everyone there. The henna that showed that their hands were clean and carefully disinfected stained their fingers brown like tobacco juice, but it smelt sweet and spicy.

"Will it rain on Saturday?" I asked the old men.

A very old man, his wrinkled face hidden behind an enormous white beard, cackled with laughter.

"No, it will not rain then," he assured me. "The sun will be out when we go and stand by the dam with the government. Many villages will be there. It will bring much honour to our doors and to the door of the research station. We will all rejoice together and the gods will be pleased."

As soon as I awoke on Saturday I pattered over to the window and raised the blind to see what the weather was like. The red soil was transformed by the sudden green growth of plants that had suddenly sprung forth from the earth. The trees looked clean and shining and the whole world smelt of the brightness of the sun when it makes its first appearance after rain. There was no doubt but that it was going to be a lovely day, and I wondered how the old man had known, but perhaps wishing had made it so, just for once, a tiny miracle for me to remember as one of my last memories of India. For I had to go, I knew that now. I could no longer listen through the nights for Julie to come to bed, nor could I smile any more when she teased and scolded Gideon at meal-times, showing me more clearly every day how confident she was of his approval and—I had to face it some time—his love for her.

I stood at the window and thought back to when I had walked back from the metalsmith with Gideon.

"You look pale," he had said. "Is there something wrong?"

I had swallowed.

"We can't all be beautiful!" I had responded miserably.

He had looked me straight in the eyes and had said : "I have always believed that beauty was largely in the eye of the beholder. Wouldn't you say that, Miss King?"

Miss King again!

"No, I don't!" I had exclaimed bitterly. "I think some people can always attract by their looks no matter what they are, and other—and others can only stand by and watch!"

He had looked rather pleased with himself and had grinned.

"Are you hinting at something, Suki?" he had asked.

I had pursed up my lips and had looked disapproving, knowing that that way I looked my plainest.

"I should have thought it was obvious!" I had said. "But you know your own business best! *I* should have thought she was most unreliable!"

And he had grinned all the harder.

"Now would you indeed?" was all he had said, and I hadn't seen him alone since then. But he had continued to flirt with Julie, that I knew, because I knew the time that she came to bed, and it wasn't Joseph who kept her company out on the verandah!

I sighed and turned away to wake up Camilla. She gave a grunt of dismay when she saw the time and leaped out of bed.

"I promised Joe I'd help him with the bunting," she explained as she tore into her clothing and fussed over her make-up. "Suki, did you know there's to be a proper ceremony and that you're to be the centre of it?"

"Well, a ceremony," I amended. "But it's only someone from the government who is coming to inspect it."

Camilla applied her lipstick with care.

"Joseph says—" she began, her eyes twinkling. "No, perhaps I'd better not tell you what he said! But look out for Julie's wrath, won't you? Something tells me she's not going to enjoy today very much."

"I don't suppose she will," I said. "Do you think Gideon will want her to be on the platform?"

Camilla flicked her hair into position and made a face at herself in the looking-glass.

"I'm beginning to wonder if he cares what happens to her," she said flatly.

"But he must do!" I exclaimed.

Camilla threw me a brief kiss as she departed.

"I don't see why! He's no fool, my brother. Hadn't

you better get ready? Don't forget that on this occasion it's you who is to be queen of the ball!"

I watched her disappear out of the door, still sitting on the edge of my bed. Then I shook my head. It was too much to hope for that Gideon should have seen through Julie. Why should he when she was always as sweet as pie as far as he was concerned? But Camilla's warning made me feel uncomfortable all the same. I could have wished that there was going to be no ceremony if Julie was going to spoil it for me.

I wore my very best dress and managed to make my unruly hair look respectable and even quite pretty. There was nothing I could do to make my face look pretty, but I was not displeased with my efforts. If I couldn't compete with Julie's fair looks, it was better to be cast in a different mould rather than an also-ran in hers. By the time I had jammed a hat on, I thought I looked quite competitive in any society.

Joseph had already gone to the railway station to get the government official when I made my appearance on the verandah. Gideon rose slowly to his feet and came towards me.

"Very nice!" he said quietly, for my benefit alone.

I blushed and he smiled at me. Julie stood up also and came languidly across the verandah.

"My dear!" she began in a soft, drawling voice. "Do you think that hat is quite suitable?"

"I wouldn't have it on if I didn't!" I retorted with a sudden spurt of temper.

She pouted. "We-ell, if you really think so—" She paused, slowly pulling on her gloves. "My parents are coming to see the fun," she told me. "Gideon asked them!"

I was glad of my hat. I could hide behind the brim and pretend I didn't care who was going to be there. But I was worried. I looked down at Gideon's leg and then out to the waiting jeep.

"Is it time to go?" I asked.

It was natural that Julie should sit in the front with Gideon. He was driving himself again now, providing he didn't go too fast so that he had to jam on the brakes in a hurry, and I was glad to have the opportunity to hold on to my hat in the wind. I was nervous and I was hoping that it didn't show, because Julie looked every inch as if she were accustomed to this sort of thing every day of her life.

The village band, led by a begging blind man who could play the *sitar* almost to perfection, was already in position, sitting on the bank of the reservoir and playing all the best-known songs in answer to the various requests from the onlookers. And there were so many onlookers! They stretched all the way from the concrete heart of the dam that at last blocked the waters, allowing various channels to gush through man-made gates that would eventually control the waters altogether, right down the banks that we had so laboriously made and across the muddy, newly planted fields from which we were hoping so much.

"They'll trample the crops!" I said in dismay.

Gideon grinned at me.

"They won't do much harm. They're all farming folk." He turned and took me by the hand. "You'd better take your place on the platform. They're waiting for you."

Julie stepped down from the jeep ahead of me. She put her arm possessively round Gideon's, pulling him away. With infinite patience he released himself.

"Sorry, Julie. You'd better find your parents and see that they're comfortable. I'm on duty today and so is Susan. I'll see you later."

Julie gave me a spiteful look.

"She shouldn't be here at all!" she protested. "I think it's ridiculous to make all this fuss over her. *You're* the man behind it all!"

But Gideon only ignored her.

"Are you ready?" he asked me grimly. I took his

hand and jumped down beside him and, without a further glance in Julie's direction, he led me towards the official space that was reserved for us.

"Do you think we ought to just leave her?" I asked anxiously.

Gideon's hand tightened on my elbow. "Why not?" he replied briefly.

He hurried me up the bank towards the dam with a fierce determination. I could hardly keep up in my high-heeled shoes and I was breathless as well as anxious by the time we had gained the top of the bank. I looked back over my shoulder to where Julie was still standing by the jeep. To my relief she waved to us and I was sure that she had forgotten her spite.

"She'll be all right," Gideon said roughly. "Don't worry about her. I'll see she doesn't bother you."

"But—" I protested.

He stopped and looked down at me and his expression was very gentle.

"I told you not to worry," he said. "I'll see she doesn't bother you."

I have to admit that I forgot all about her as we reached the little clearing on the top of the bank. The old men of the *panchayat* stood in a little semi-circle overlooking the rapidly filling reservoir. We greeted them individually, one by one, putting the palms of our hands together in the traditional Indian greeting and then shaking them warmly by the hand. We were only halfway through this little ceremony when the *Swami* came striding through the crowds towards us. His wild, matted hair stood straight on end and his orange robe seemed to hide less of him even than usual, but his air of authority was as strong as ever. As soon as he had come up with us, he sank on to the ground, apparently oblivious of everyone around us, and contemplated a small patch of ground in front of him. Nobody paid the faintest attention to him. They knew he would join us when he was ready.

I could see the approaching jeep bringing the government official from a long way off. Joseph and Camilla had hung it about with scarlet bunting and the Indian flag flew from the windscreen, proudly declaring that this was an official occasion. The crowd, completely silent as Indian crowds so often are, made room for the vehicle to pass, peering over one another's shoulders to look at the occupant to see what he looked like. I found myself as eager as every one else to see him and I took a quick step forward, almost tripping over the *Swami*.

"I'm so sorry," I apologised, but apparently he hadn't noticed.

"Where's Camilla?" Gideon asked me urgently.

I peered down at the jeep coming towards us.

"Isn't she with Joseph?"

He shook his head.

"Never mind, we haven't time to look for her now. I'll go down and welcome our guest if you and the *Swami* will wait here and keep things moving."

The *Swami* awoke from his dream and stood up. He came over and stood beside me, smiling gently.

"I think this is as much your great day as it is the village's," he commented gravely. "You have made yourself very much one of us. A lot of people would be sad if you were to leave us now—Lakshmi particularly. She tells me you were instrumental in her becoming engaged to some young man?"

I blushed.

"Hardly," I replied, embarrassed by his approval. "All I did was to mention it to Gideon."

He smiled his acknowledgment.

"And that was enough," he agreed. "Nevertheless she is very happy at the outcome."

He turned away to chat to the old men around him, but at that moment Julie came running up the bank towards us, her face white and looking really frightened.

"It's my father!" she gasped. She flinched away from

the *Swami* and turned to me. "He's fallen in the water," she said. "It was all a joke! He only wanted to see that Gideon got his fair share of the credit. He didn't see why you should be standing up here, any more than I could. He was going to make sure that the government man was taken round the other way and didn't see you at all. And then Camilla pushed him in!"

"Camilla did?" My first reaction was to want to burst out laughing, and even the *Swami* looked amused. Julie stamped her foot at the two of us.

"He *can't swim*!"

I caught some of her fright at that. I took off my high-heeled shoes and left them on the top of the bank and ran after her to the other side of the stream and up the other bank to where she thought her father was. A little knot of people had gathered on the edge of the water, giggling and nudging one another. I pushed my way through them and ran straight into Gideon's waiting arms.

"My goodness," he said in an amused voice, "we don't want to have two of you all wet and dripping. Where are you going in such a hurry?"

I tried to release myself from his clasp, but he didn't appear to notice. In fact he held me all the closer as though he didn't want to let me go.

"I thought he might have hurt you," I said at last in shaken tones.

Gideon shook his head. "Not twice," he said grimly.

"But what happened?" I asked.

A tiny, birdlike man, dressed in a *dhoti* and a Congress cap, came forward and shook my hand.

"It was very sudden. This man tried to kidnap me, I am sure of it! He kept saying he wished to introduce me to Mr. Wait's finacée. Then this girl pushed him into the water!" He waved a hand to where Camilla was standing.

Despite myself, I giggled. Gideon's clasp tightened round my waist.

"Suki, my love, take Mr. Singh and introduce him to the *panchayat*, will you? I'll wrap Mr. Burnett in a blanket and Julie can take him home to his loving wife!"

"I won't!" Julie cried out desperately. "I'm staying here. You *asked* me to stay!"

"And now I am asking you to go," Gideon replied calmly. "Your father will be better off at home in his own dream world of an existence."

Julie said nothing at all. She tore at his arm and tried to pull him towards her.

"I'm not coming, Julie," he said.

"But why not?" she demanded. She turned on me bitterly. "It's because of you! Isn't it? I suppose you think you can fascinate him with a few grains of wheat for ever!"

But somehow no one was listening to her. Gideon wrapped Mr. Burnett up in a rug from the jeep, pushed him into the vehicle and lifted Julie in beside him.

"Drive them back to their car," he ordered Joseph briefly.

Camilla jumped up and down impatiently.

"I'll go with him and bring him back safe and sound!" she announced.

Gideon grinned at her. "Okay," he said. "Just so long as Suki stays here with me."

The band was still playing when we arrived back at our reserved positions. I felt a little self-conscious without my shoes and I was horribly aware of Gideon's amusement when the *Swami* silently held them out to me. It was Gideon, though, who put them on for me.

"Well, Mr. Singh," he drawled as he stood up, "what do you think of our dam?"

The government official beamed his approval. From somewhere in his *dhoti* he produced the notes of his speech. The band was silent and he began to speak.

I have no idea what he said. Gideon and I stood a little behind him. He held my hand tightly in his and

I stood in a dream, wondering what I had done to deserve such happiness.

It seemed a very long time before Mr. Singh came to an end of his speech, but I didn't care. Even when the clouds came rolling back and more rain threatened to spoil the brightness of the day, it didn't seem to matter. And then, from nowhere, Mr. Singh produced a garland of marigolds and placed it carefully round my neck.

"The marigold means much to us," he said. "It is the colour of the rising sun and the beginning of the dawn of understanding."

There were garlands for everyone. Splashes of orange spread through the crowds. The band began to play again and the crowds broke into song. It was very pretty and it made me want to cry.

"I think we can go," Gideon whispered in my ear. "Will you come home with me?"

I nodded. I couldn't have spoken at that moment. It was as if I had never seen him before, and I knew with a trembling certainty that he knew it too. People stood aside as we slithered down the bank and commandeered the first vehicle we came to. Gideon helped me in, smiling at my uncertainty in my high-heeled shoes.

"Darling, could you take that garland off?" he asked me humorously.

I clutched it to me, admiring the clever way it had been made.

"Why?" I asked. "I'm very proud of it!"

He laughed. "I guess I am too," he admitted.

He sat beside me and drove the jeep off at a great pace until we had left the dam and the crowds far behind us. The first drops of rain were beginning to fall again. Great drops of warm water as big as cherries splattered on to the metal bonnet. When it began to rain in earnest, I thought, we wouldn't be able to hear what we were saying.

"Darling," he said, and he already had to shout, "do you love me?"

But I couldn't say it.

"Was it a mistake to be kind to Julie?" he asked. "She was an awful nuisance to me the whole time she was here!"

"I know," I said. "I saw it in your face when you told her to go."

He pulled me a little closer to him.

"And you love me?" he asked again. But he gave me no time to answer. His mouth came down on mine and I was lost in his arms. The pungent smell of crushed marigolds mixed with the rain.

"Yes," I said when I could. "I love you! I love you! *I love you!*"

And he kissed me again.

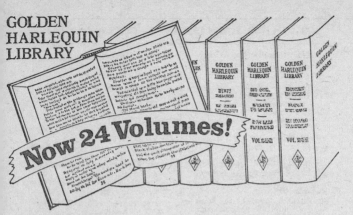

GOLDEN HARLEQUIN LIBRARY

Now 24 Volumes!

Harlequin readers will be delighted! We've collected seventy two of your all-time favourite Harlequin Romance novels to present to you in an attractive new way. It's the Golden Harlequin Library.

Each volume contains three complete, unabridged Harlequin Romance novels, most of which have not been available since the original printing. Each volume is exquisitely bound in a fine quality rich gold hardcover with royal blue imprint. And each volume is priced at an unbelievable $1.75. That's right! Handsome, hardcover library editions at the price of paperbacks!

This very special collection of 24 volumes (there'll be more!) of classic Harlequin Romances would be a distinctive addition to your library. And imagine what a delightful gift they'd make for any Harlequin reader!

Start your collection now. See reverse of this page for full details.

GOLDEN HARLEQUIN LIBRARY — $1.75 each volume

Special Introductory Offer
(First 6 volumes only $8.75)

☐ **VOLUME I**
  692 THE ONLY CHARITY, Sara Seale
  785 THE SURGEON'S MARRIAGE
     Kathryn Blair
  806 THE GOLDEN PEAKS
     Eleanor Farnes

☐ **VOLUME II**
  649 KATE OF OUTPATIENTS
     Elizabeth Gilzean
  774 HEATHERLEIGH, Essie Summers
  853 SUGAR ISLAND, Jean S. Macleod

☐ **VOLUME III**
  506 QUEEN'S COUNSEL, Alex Stuart
  760 FAIR HORIZON, Rosalind Brett
  801 DESERT NURSE, Jane Arbor

☐ **VOLUME IV**
  501 DO SOMETHING DANGEROUS
     Elizabeth Hoy
  816 THE YOUNGEST BRIDESMAID
     Sara Seale
  875 DOCTOR DAVID ADVISES
     Hilary Wilde

☐ **VOLUME V**
  721 SHIP'S SURGEON, Celine Conway
  862 MOON OVER THE ALPS
     Essie Summers
  887 LAKE OF SHADOWS, Jane Arbor

☐ **VOLUME VI**
  644 NEVER TO LOVE, Anne Weale
  650 THE GOLDEN ROSE, Kathryn Blair
  814 A LONG WAY FROM HOME
     Jane Fraser

Just Published
($1.75 per volume)

☐ **VOLUME XIX**
  705 THE LAST OF THE LOGANS
     Alex Stuart
  740 NURSE ON HOLIDAY
     Rosalind Brett
  789 COUNTRY OF THE HEART
     Catherine Airlie

☐ **VOLUME XX**
  594 DOCTOR SARA COMES HOME
     Elizabeth Houghton
  603 ACROSS THE COUNTER
     Mary Burchell
  736 THE TALL PINES, Celine Conway

☐ **VOLUME XXI**
  716 THE DOCTOR'S DAUGHTERS
     Anne Weale
  792 GATES OF DAWN, Susan Barrie
  808 THE GIRL AT SNOWY RIVER
     Joyce Dingwell

☐ **VOLUME XXII**
  524 QUEEN'S NURSE, Jane Arbor
  725 THE SONG AND THE SEA
     Isobel Chace
  791 CITY OF PALMS, Pamela Kent

☐ **VOLUME XXIII**
  742 COME BLOSSOM-TIME, MY LOVE
     Essie Summers
  778 A CASE IN THE ALPS
     Margaret Baumann
  848 THE KEEPER'S HOUSE
     Jane Fraser

☐ **VOLUME XXIV**
  560 WINTERSBRIDE, Sara Seale
  592 MARRIAGE COMPROMISE
     Margaret Malcolm
  700 TAMARISK BAY, Kathryn Blair

To: Harlequin Reader Service, Dept. G.
    M.P.O. Box 707, Niagara Falls, N.Y. 14302
    Canadian address: Stratford, Ont., Canada

☐ Please send me complete listing of the 24 Golden Harlequin Library Volumes.

☐ Please send me the Golden Harlequin Library editions I have indicated above.

I enclose $............................ (No C.O.D.'s) To help defray postage and handling costs, please add 50c.

Name ....

Address ....

City/Town ....

State/Province .... Zip.................................